Louis Lambert

Honoré de Balzac

Louis Lambert

Copyright © 2024 Indo-European Publishing

The present edition is a reproduction of previous publication of this classic work. Minor typographical errors may have been corrected without note; however, for an authentic reading experience the spelling, punctuation, and capitalization have been retained from the original text.

ISBN: 979-8-88942-392-8

CONTENTS

LOUIS LAMBERT

DEDICATION

"Et nunc et semper dilectoe dicatum"

Louis Lambert was born at Montoire, a little town in the Vendomois, where his father owned a tannery of no great magnitude, and intended that his son should succeed him; but his precocious bent for study modified the paternal decision. For, indeed, the tanner and his wife adored Louis, their only child, and never contradicted him in anything.

At the age of five Louis had begun by reading the Old and New Testaments; and these two Books, including so many books, had sealed his fate. Could that childish imagination understand the mystical depths of the Scriptures? Could it so early follow the flight of the Holy Spirit across the worlds? Or was it merely attracted by the romantic touches which abound in those Oriental poems! Our narrative will answer these questions to some readers.

One thing resulted from this first reading of the Bible: Louis went all over Montoire begging for books, and he obtained them by those winning ways peculiar to children, which no one can resist. While devoting himself to these studies under no sort of guidance, he reached the age of ten.

At that period substitutes for the army were scarce; rich families secured them long beforehand to have them ready when the lots were drawn. The poor tanner's modest fortune did not allow of their purchasing a substitute for their son, and they saw no means allowed by law for evading the conscription but that of making him a priest; so, in 1807, they sent him to his maternal uncle, the parish priest of Mer, another small town on the Loire, not far from Blois. This arrangement at once satisfied Louis' passion for knowledge, and his parents' wish not to expose him to the dreadful chances of war; and, indeed, his taste for study and precocious intelligence gave grounds for hoping that he might rise to high fortunes in the Church.

After remaining for about three years with his uncle, an old and not uncultured Oratorian, Louis left him early in 1811 to enter the college at Vendome, where he was maintained at the cost of Madame de Stael.

Lambert owed the favor and patronage of this celebrated lady to chance, or shall we not say to Providence, who can smooth the path of forlorn genius? To us, indeed, who do not see below the surface of human things, such vicissitudes, of which we find many examples in the lives of great men, appear to be merely the result of physical phenomena; to most biographers the head of a man of genius rises above the herd as some noble plant in the fields attracts the eye of a botanist in its splendor. This comparison may well be applied to Louis Lambert's adventure; he was accustomed to spend the time allowed him by his uncle for holidays at his father's house; but instead of indulging, after the manner of schoolboys, in the sweets of the delightful far niente that tempts us at every age, he set out every morning with part of a loaf and his books, and went to read and meditate in the woods, to escape his mother's remonstrances, for she believed such persistent study to be injurious. How admirable is a mother's instinct! From that time reading was in Louis a sort of appetite which nothing could satisfy; he devoured books of every kind, feeding indiscriminately on religious works, history, philosophy, and physics. He has told me that he found indescribable delight in reading dictionaries for lack of other books, and I readily believed him. What scholar has not many a time found pleasure in seeking the probable meaning of some unknown word? The analysis of a word, its physiognomy and history, would be to Lambert matter for long dreaming. But these were not the instinctive dreams by which a boy accustoms himself to the phenomena of life, steels himself to every moral or physical perception—an involuntary education which subsequently brings forth fruit both in the understanding and character of a man; no, Louis mastered the facts, and he accounted for them after seeking out both the principle and the end with the mother wit of a savage. Indeed, from the age of fourteen, by one of those startling freaks in which nature sometimes indulges, and which proved how anomalous was his temperament, he would utter quite simply ideas of which the depth was not revealed to me till a long time after.

"Often," he has said to me when speaking of his studies, "often have I made the most delightful voyage, floating on a word down the abyss of the past, like an insect embarked on a blade of grass tossing on the ripples of a stream. Starting from Greece, I would get to Rome, and traverse the whole extent of modern ages. What a fine book might be written of the life and adventures of a word! It has, of course, received various stamps from the occasions on which it has served its purpose; it has conveyed different ideas in different places; but is it not still grander to think of it under the three aspects of soul, body, and motion? Merely to regard it in the abstract, apart from its functions, its effects, and its influence, is enough to cast one into an ocean of meditations? Are not most words colored by the idea they represent? Then, to whose genius are they due? If it takes great intelligence to create a word, how old may human speech be? The combination of letters, their shapes, and the look they give to the word, are the exact reflection, in accordance with the character of each nation, of the unknown beings whose traces survive in us.

"Who can philosophically explain the transition from sensation to thought, from thought to word, from the word to its hieroglyphic presentment, from hieroglyphics to the alphabet, from the alphabet to written language, of which the eloquent beauty resides in a series of images, classified by rhetoric, and forming, in a sense, the hieroglyphics of thought? Was it not the ancient mode of representing human ideas as embodied in the forms of animals that gave rise to the shapes of the first signs used in the East for writing down language? Then has it not left its traces by tradition on our modern languages, which have all seized some remnant of the primitive speech of nations, a majestic and solemn tongue whose grandeur and solemnity decrease as communities grow old; whose sonorous tones ring in the Hebrew Bible, and still are noble in Greece, but grow weaker under the progress of successive phases of civilization?

"Is it to this time-honored spirit that we owe the mysteries lying buried in every human word? In the word True do we not discern a certain imaginary rectitude? Does not the compact brevity of its sound suggest a vague image of chaste nudity and the simplicity of Truth in all things? The syllable seems to me singularly crisp and fresh.

"I chose the formula of an abstract idea on purpose, not wishing to illustrate the case by a word which should make it too obvious to the apprehension, as the word Flight for instance, which is a direct appeal to the senses.

"But is it not so with every root word? They are all stamped with a living power that comes from the soul, and which they restore to the soul through the mysterious and wonderful action and reaction between thought and speech. Might we not speak of it as a lover who finds on his mistress' lips as much love as he gives? Thus, by their mere physiognomy, words call to life in our brain the beings which they serve to clothe. Like all beings, there is but one place where their properties are at full liberty to act and develop. But the subject demands a science to itself perhaps!"

And he would shrug his shoulders as much as to say, "But we are too high and too low!"

Louis' passion for reading had on the whole been very well satisfied. The cure of Mer had two or three thousand volumes. This treasure had been derived from the plunder committed during the Revolution in the neighboring chateaux and abbeys. As a priest who had taken the oath, the worthy man had been able to choose the best books from among these precious libraries, which were sold by the pound. In three years Louis Lambert had assimilated the contents of all the books in his uncle's library that were worth reading. The process of absorbing ideas by means of reading had become in him a very strange phenomenon. His eye took in six or seven lines at once, and his mind grasped the sense with a swiftness as remarkable as that of his eye; sometimes even one word in a sentence was enough to enable him to seize the gist of the matter.

His memory was prodigious. He remembered with equal exactitude the ideas he had derived from reading, and those which had occurred to him in the course of meditation or conversation. Indeed, he had every form of memory—for places, for names, for words, things, and faces. He not only recalled any object at will, but he saw them in his mind, situated, lighted, and colored as he had originally seen them. And this power he could exert with equal effect with regard to the most abstract efforts of the intellect. He could remember, as he said, not merely the position of a sentence in the book where he had met with it, but the frame of mind he had been in at remote dates. Thus his was the singular privilege of being able to retrace in memory the whole life and progress of his mind, from the ideas he had first acquired to the last thought evolved in it, from the most obscure to the clearest. His brain, accustomed in early youth to the mysterious mechanism by which human faculties are concentrated, drew from this rich treasury endless images full of life and freshness, on which he fed his spirit during those lucid spells of contemplation.

"Whenever I wish it," said he to me in his own language, to which a fund of remembrance gave precocious originality, "I can draw a veil over my eyes. Then I suddenly see within me a camera obscura, where natural objects are reproduced in purer forms than those under which they first appeared to my external sense."

At the age of twelve his imagination, stimulated by the perpetual exercise of his faculties, had developed to a point which permitted him to have such precise concepts of things which he knew only from reading about them, that the image stamped on his mind could not have been clearer if he had actually seen them, whether this was by a process of analogy or that he was gifted with a sort of second sight by which he could command all nature.

"When I read the story of the battle of Austerlitz," said he to me one day, "I saw every incident. The roar of the cannon, the cries of the fighting men rang in my ears, and made my inmost self quiver; I could smell the powder; I heard the clatter of horses and the voices of men; I looked down on the plain where armed nations were in collision, just as if I had been on the heights of Santon. The scene was as terrifying as a passage from the Apocalypse." On the occasions when he brought all his powers into play, and in some degree lost consciousness of his physical existence, and lived on only by the remarkable energy of his mental powers, whose sphere was enormously expanded, he left space behind him, to use his own words.

But I will not here anticipate the intellectual phases of his life. Already, in spite of myself, I have reversed the order in which I ought to tell the history of this man, who transferred all his activities to thinking, as others throw all their life into action.

A strong bias drew his mind into mystical studies.

"Abyssus abyssum," he would say. "Our spirit is abysmal and

loves the abyss. In childhood, manhood, and old age we are always eager for mysteries in whatever form they present themselves."

This predilection was disastrous; if indeed his life can be measured by ordinary standards, or if we may gauge another's happiness by our own or by social notions. This taste for the "things of heaven," another phrase he was fond of using, this mens divinior, was due perhaps to the influence produced on his mind by the first books he read at his uncle's. Saint Theresa and Madame Guyon were a sequel to the Bible; they had the first-fruits of his manly intelligence, and accustomed him to those swift reactions of the soul of which ecstasy is at once the result and the means. This line of study, this peculiar taste, elevated his heart, purified, ennobled it, gave him an appetite for the divine nature, and suggested to him the almost womanly refinement of feeling which is instinctive in great men; perhaps their sublime superiority is no more than the desire to devote themselves which characterizes woman, only transferred to the greatest things.

As a result of these early impressions, Louis passed immaculate through his school life; this beautiful virginity of the senses naturally resulted in the richer fervor of his blood, and in increased faculties of mind.

The Baroness de Stael, forbidden to come within forty leagues of Paris, spent several months of her banishment on an estate near Vendome. One day, when out walking, she met on the skirts of the park the tanner's son, almost in rags, and absorbed in reading. The book was a translation of Heaven and Hell. At that time Monsieur Saint-Martin, Monsieur de Gence, and a few other French or half German writers were almost the only persons in the French Empire to whom the name of Swedenborg was known. Madame de Stael, greatly surprised, took the book from him with the roughness she affected in her questions, looks, and manners, and with a keen glance at Lambert,—

"Do you understand all this?" she asked.

"Do you pray to God?" said the child.

"Why? yes!"

"And do you understand Him?"

The Baroness was silent for a moment; then she sat down by Lambert, and began to talk to him. Unfortunately, my memory, though retentive, is far from being so trustworthy as my friend's, and I have forgotten the whole of the dialogue excepting those first words.

Such a meeting was of a kind to strike Madame de Stael very greatly; on her return home she said but little about it, notwithstanding an effusiveness which in her became mere loquacity; but it evidently occupied her thoughts.

The only person now living who preserves any recollection of the incident, and whom I catechised to be informed of what few words Madame de Stael had let drop, could with difficulty recall these words spoken by the Baroness as describing Lambert, "He is a real seer."

Louis failed to justify in the eyes of the world the high hopes he had inspired in his protectress. The transient favor she showed him was regarded as a feminine caprice, one of the fancies characteristic of artist souls. Madame de Stael determined to save Louis Lambert alike from serving the Emperor or the Church, and to preserve him for the glorious destiny which, she thought, awaited him; for she made him out to be a second Moses snatched from the waters. Before her departure she instructed a friend of hers, Monsieur de Corbigny, to send her Moses in due course to the High School at Vendome; then she probably forgot him.

Having entered this college at the age of fourteen, early in 1811, Lambert would leave it at the end of 1814, when he had finished the course of Philosophy. I doubt whether during the whole time he ever heard a word of his benefactress—if indeed it was the act of a benefactress to pay for a lad's schooling for three years without a thought of his future prospects, after diverting him from a career in which he might have found happiness. The circumstances of the time, and Louis Lambert's character, may to a great extent absolve Madame de Stael for her thoughtlessness and her generosity. The gentleman who was to have kept up communications between her and the boy left Blois just at the time when Louis passed out of the college. The political events that ensued were then a sufficient excuse for this gentleman's neglect of the Baroness' protege. The authoress of Corinne heard no more of her little Moses.

A hundred louis, which she placed in the hands of Monsieur de Corbigny, who died, I believe, in 1812, was not a sufficiently large sum to leave lasting memories in Madame de Stael, whose excitable nature found ample pasture during the vicissitudes of 1814 and 1815, which absorbed all her interest.

At this time Louis Lambert was at once too proud and too poor to go in search of a patroness who was traveling all over Europe. However, he went on foot from Blois to Paris in the hope of seeing her, and arrived, unluckily, on the very day of her death. Two letters from Lambert to the Baroness remained unanswered. The memory of Madame de Stael's good intentions with regard to Louis remains, therefore, only in some few young minds, struck, as mine was, by the strangeness of the story.

No one who had not gone through the training at our college could understand the effect usually made on our minds by the announcement that a "new boy" had arrived, or the impression that such an adventure as Louis Lambert's was calculated to produce.

And here a little information must be given as to the primitive administration of this institution, originally half-military and half-monastic, to explain the new life which there awaited Lambert. Before the Revolution, the Oratorians, devoted, like the Society of Jesus, to the education of youth—succeeding the Jesuits, in fact, in certain of their establishments—the colleges of Vendome, of Tournon, of la Fleche, Pont-Levoy, Sorreze, and Juilly. That at Vendome, like the others, I believe, turned out a certain number of cadets for the army. The abolition of educational bodies, decreed by the convention, had but little effect on the college at Vendome. When the first crisis had blown over, the authorities recovered possession of their buildings; certain Oratorians, scattered about the country, came back to the college and re-opened it under the old rules, with the habits, practices, and customs which gave this school a character with which I have seen nothing at all comparable in any that I have visited since I left that establishment.

Standing in the heart of the town, on the little river Loire which flows under its walls, the college possesses extensive precincts, carefully enclosed by walls, and including all the buildings necessary for an institution on that scale: a chapel, a theatre, an infirmary, a bakehouse, gardens, and water supply. This college is the most celebrated home of learning in all the central provinces, and receives pupils from them and from the colonies. Distance prohibits any frequent visits from parents to their children.

The rule of the House forbids holidays away from it. Once entered there, a pupil never leaves till his studies are finished. With the exception of walks taken under the guidance of the Fathers, everything is calculated to give the School the benefit of conventual discipline; in my day the tawse was still a living memory, and the classical leather strap played its terrible part with all the honors. The punishment originally invented by the Society of Jesus, as alarming to the moral as to the physical man, was still in force in all the integrity of the original code.

Letters to parents were obligatory on certain days, so was confession. Thus our sins and our sentiments were all according to pattern. Everything bore the stamp of monastic rule. I well remember, among other relics of the ancient order, the inspection we went through every Sunday. We were all in our best, placed in file like soldiers to await the arrival of the two inspectors who, attended by the tutors and the tradesmen, examined us from the three points of view of dress, health, and morals.

The two or three hundred pupils lodged in the establishment were divided, according to ancient custom, into the minimes (the smallest), the little boys, the middle boys, and the big boys. The division of the minimes included the eighth and seventh classes; the little boys formed the sixth, fifth, and fourth; the middle boys were classed as third and second; and the first class comprised the senior students—of philosophy, rhetoric, the higher mathematics, and chemistry. Each of these divisions had its own building, classrooms, and play-ground, in the large common precincts on to which the classrooms opened, and beyond which was the refectory.

This dining-hall, worthy of an ancient religious Order, accommodated all the school. Contrary to the usual practice in educational institutions, we were allowed to talk at our meals, a tolerant Oratorian rule which enabled us to exchange plates according to our taste. This gastronomical barter was always one of the chief pleasures of our college life. If one of the "middle" boys at the head of his table wished for a helping of lentils instead of dessert—for we had dessert—the offer was passed down from one to another: "Dessert for lentils!" till some other epicure had accepted; then the plate of lentils was passed up to the bidder from hand to hand, and the plate of dessert returned by the same road. Mistakes were never made. If several identical offers were made, they were taken in order, and the formula would be, "Lentils number one for dessert number one." The tables were very long; our incessant barter kept everything moving; we transacted it with amazing eagerness; and the chatter of three hundred lads, the bustling to and fro of the servants employed in changing the plates, setting down the dishes, handing the bread, with the tours of inspection of the masters, made this refectory at Vendome a scene unique in its way, and the amazement of visitors.

To make our life more tolerable, deprived as we were of all communication with the outer world and of family affection, we were allowed to keep pigeons and to have gardens. Our two or three hundred pigeon-houses, with a thousand birds nesting all round the outer wall, and above thirty garden plots, were a sight even stranger than our meals. But a full account of the peculiarities which made the college at Vendome a place unique in itself and fertile in reminiscences to those who spent their boyhood there, would be weariness to the reader. Which of us all but remembers with delight, notwithstanding the bitterness of learning, the eccentric pleasures of that cloistered life? The sweetmeats purchased by stealth in the course of our walks, permission obtained to play cards and devise theatrical performances during the holidays, such tricks and freedom as were necessitated by our seclusion; then, again, our military band, a relic of the cadets; our academy, our chaplain, our Father professors, and all our games permitted or prohibited, as the case might be; the cavalry charges on stilts, the long slides made in winter, the clatter of our clogs; and, above all, the trading transactions with "the shop" set up in the courtyard itself.

This shop was kept by a sort of cheap-jack, of whom big and

little boys could procure—according to his prospectus—boxes, stilts, tools, Jacobin pigeons, and Nuns, Mass-books—an article in small demand —penknives, paper, pens, pencils, ink of all colors, balls and marbles; in short, the whole catalogue of the most treasured possessions of boys, including everything from sauce for the pigeons we were obliged to kill off, to the earthenware pots in which we set aside the rice from supper to be eaten at next morning's breakfast. Which of us was so unhappy as to have forgotten how his heart beat at the sight of this booth, open periodically during play-hours on Sundays, to which we went, each in his turn, to spend his little pocket-money; while the smallness of the sum allowed by our parents for these minor pleasures required us to make a choice among all the objects that appealed so strongly to our desires? Did ever a young wife, to whom her husband, during the first days of happiness, hands, twelve times a year, a purse of gold, the budget of her personal fancies, dream of so many different purchases, each of which would absorb the whole sum, as we imagined possible on the eve of the first Sunday in each month? For six francs during one night we owned every delight of that inexhaustible shop! and during Mass every response we chanted was mixed up in our minds with our secret calculations. Which of us all can recollect ever having had a sou left to spend on the Sunday following? And which of us but obeyed the instinctive law of social existence by pitying, helping, and despising those pariahs who, by the avarice or poverty of their parents, found themselves penniless?

Any one who forms a clear idea of this huge college, with its monastic buildings in the heart of a little town, and the four plots in which we were distributed as by a monastic rule, will easily conceive of the excitement that we felt at the arrival of a new boy, a passenger suddenly embarked on the ship. No young duchess, on her first appearance at Court, was ever more spitefully criticised than the new boy by the youths in his division. Usually during the evening play-hour before prayers, those sycophants who were accustomed to ingratiate themselves with the Fathers who took it in turns two and two for a week to keep an eye on us, would be the first to hear on trustworthy authority: "There will be a new boy to-morrow!" and then suddenly the shout, "A New Boy!—A New Boy!" rang through the courts. We hurried up to crowd round the superintendent and pester him with questions:

"Where was he coming from? What was his name? Which class would he be in?" and so forth.

Louis Lambert's advent was the subject of a romance worthy of the Arabian Nights. I was in the fourth class at the time—among the little boys. Our housemasters were two men whom we called Fathers from habit and tradition, though they were not priests. In my time there were indeed but three genuine Oratorians to whom this title legitimately belonged; in 1814 they all left the college, which had gradually become secularized, to find occupation about the altar in various country parishes, like the cure of Mer.

Father Haugoult, the master for the week, was not a bad man, but of very moderate attainments, and he lacked the tact which is indispensable for discerning the different characters of children, and graduating their punishment to their powers of resistance. Father Haugoult, then, began very obligingly to communicate to his pupils the wonderful events which were to end on the morrow in the advent of the most singular of "new boys." Games were at an end. All the children came round in silence to hear the story of Louis Lambert, discovered, like an aerolite, by Madame de Stael, in a corner of the wood. Monsieur Haugoult had to tell us all about Madame de Stael; that evening she seemed to me ten feet high; I saw at a later time the picture of Corinne, in which Gerard represents her as so tall and handsome; and, alas! the woman painted by my imagination so far transcended this, that the real Madame de Stael fell at once in my estimation, even after I read her book of really masculine power, De l'Allemagne.

But Lambert at that time was an even greater wonder. Monsieur Mareschal, the headmaster, after examining him, had thought of placing him among the senior boys. It was Louis' ignorance of Latin that placed him so low as the fourth class, but he would certainly leap up a class every year; and, as a remarkable exception, he was to be one of the "Academy." Proh pudor! we were to have the honor of counting among the "little boys" one whose coat was adorned with the red ribbon displayed by the

"Academicians" of Vendome. These Academicians enjoyed distinguished privileges; they often dined at the director's table, and held two literary meetings annually, at which we were all present to hear their elucubrations. An Academician was a great man in embryo. And if every Vendome scholar would speak the truth, he would confess that, in later life, an Academician of the great French Academy seemed to him far less remarkable than the stupendous boy who wore the cross and the imposing red ribbon which were the insignia of our "Academy."

It was very unusual to be one of that illustrious body before attaining to the second class, for the Academicians were expected to hold public meetings every Thursday during the holidays, and to read tales in verse or prose, epistles, essays, tragedies, dramas—compositions far above the intelligence of the lower classes. I long treasured the memory of a story called the "Green Ass," which was, I think, the masterpiece of this unknown Society. In the fourth, and an Academician! This boy of fourteen, a poet already, the protege of Madame de Stael, a coming genius, said Father Haugoult, was to be one of us! a wizard, a youth capable of writing a composition or a translation while we were being called into lessons, and of learning his lessons by reading them through but once. Louis Lambert bewildered all our ideas. And Father Haugoult's curiosity and impatience to see this new boy added fuel to our excited fancy.

"If he has pigeons, he can have no pigeon-house; there is not room for another. Well, it cannot be helped," said one boy, since famous as an agriculturist.

"Who will sit next to him?" said another.

"Oh, I wish I might be his chum!" cried an enthusiast.

In school language, the word here rendered chum—faisant, or in some schools, copin—expressed a fraternal sharing of the joys and evils of your childish existence, a community of interests that was fruitful of squabbling and making friends again, a treaty of alliance offensive and defensive. It is strange, but never in my time did I know brothers who were chums. If man lives by his feelings, he thinks perhaps that he will make his life the poorer if he merges an affection of his own choosing in a natural tie.

The impression made upon me by Father Haugoult's harangue

that evening is one of the most vivid reminiscences of my childhood; I can compare it with nothing but my first reading of Robinson Crusoe. Indeed, I owe to my recollection of these prodigious impressions an observation that may perhaps be new as to the different sense attached to words by each hearer. The word in itself has no final meaning; we affect a word more than it affects us; its value is in relation to the images we have assimilated and grouped round it; but a study of this fact would require considerable elaboration, and lead us too far from our immediate subject.

Not being able to sleep, I had a long discussion with my next neighbor in the dormitory as to the remarkable being who on the morrow was to be one of us. This neighbor, who became an officer, and is now a writer with lofty philosophical views, Barchou de Penhoen, has not been false to his pre-destination, nor to the hazard of fortune by which the only two scholars of Vendome, of whose fame Vendome ever hears, were brought together in the same classroom, on the same form, and under the same roof. Our comrade Dufaure had not, when this book was published, made his appearance in public life as a lawyer. The translator of Fichte, the expositor and friend of Ballanche, was already interested, as I myself was, in metaphysical questions; we often talked nonsense together about God, ourselves, and nature. He at that time affected pyrrhonism. Jealous of his place as leader, he doubted Lambert's precocious gifts; while I, having lately read Les Enfants celebres, overwhelmed him with evidence, quoting young Montcalm, Pico della Mirandola, Pascal—in short, a score of early developed brains, anomalies that are famous in the history of the human mind, and Lambert's predecessors.

I was at the time passionately addicted to reading. My father, who was ambitious to see me in the Ecole Polytechnique, paid for me to have a special course of private lessons in mathematics. My mathematical master was the librarian of the college, and allowed me to help myself to books without much caring what I chose to take from the library, a quiet spot where I went to him during play-hours to have my lesson. Either he was no great mathematician, or he was absorbed in some grand scheme, for he very willingly left me to read when I ought to have been learning, while he worked at I knew not what. So, by a tacit understanding between us, I made no complaints of being taught nothing, and he said nothing of the books I borrowed.

Carried away by this ill-timed mania, I neglected my studies to compose poems, which certainly can have shown no great promise, to judge by a line of too many feet which became famous among my companions—the beginning of an epic on the Incas:

"O Inca! O roi infortune et malheureux!"

In derision of such attempts, I was nicknamed the Poet, but mockery did not cure me. I was always rhyming, in spite of good advice from Monsieur Mareschal, the headmaster, who tried to cure me of an unfortunately inveterate passion by telling me the fable of a linnet that fell out of the nest because it tried to fly before its wings were grown. I persisted in my reading; I became the least emulous, the idlest, the most dreamy of all the division of "little boys," and consequently the most frequently punished.

This autobiographical digression may give some idea of the reflections I was led to make in anticipation of Lambert's arrival. I was then twelve years old. I felt sympathy from the first for the boy whose temperament had some points of likeness to my own. I was at last to have a companion in daydreams and meditations. Though I knew not yet what glory meant, I thought it glory to be the familiar friend of a child whose immortality was foreseen by Madame de Stael. To me Louis Lambert was as a giant.

The looked-for morrow came at last. A minute before breakfast we heard the steps of Monsieur Mareschal and of the new boy in the quiet courtyard. Every head was turned at once to the door of the classroom. Father Haugoult, who participated in our torments of curiosity, did not sound the whistle he used to reduce our mutterings to silence and bring us back to our tasks. We then saw this famous new boy, whom Monsieur Mareschal was leading by the hand. The superintendent descended from his desk, and the headmaster said to him solemnly, according to etiquette:

"Monsieur, I have brought you Monsieur Louis Lambert; will you place him in the fourth class? He will begin work to-morrow."

Then, after speaking a few words in an undertone to the class-master, he said:

"Where can he sit?"

It would have been unfair to displace one of us for a newcomer; so as there was but one desk vacant, Louis Lambert came to fill it, next to me, for I had last joined the class. Though we still had some time to wait before lessons were over, we all stood up to look at Louis Lambert. Monsieur Mareschal heard our mutterings, saw how eager we were, and said, with the kindness that endeared him to us all:

"Well, well, but make no noise; do not disturb the other classes."

These words set us free to play some little time before breakfast, and we all gathered round Lambert while Monsieur Mareschal walked up and down the courtyard with Father Haugoult.

There were about eighty of us little demons, as bold as birds of prey. Though we ourselves had all gone through this cruel novitiate, we showed no mercy on a newcomer, never sparing him the mockery, the catechism, the impertinence, which were inexhaustible on such occasions, to the discomfiture of the neophyte, whose manners, strength, and temper were thus tested. Lambert, whether he was stoical or dumfounded, made no reply to any questions. One of us thereupon remarked that he was no doubt of the school of Pythagoras, and there was a shout of laughter. The new boy was thenceforth Pythagoras through all his life at the college. At the same time, Lambert's piercing eye, the scorn expressed in his face for our childishness, so far removed from the stamp of his own nature, the easy attitude he assumed, and his evident strength in proportion to his years, infused a certain respect into the veriest scamps among us. For my part, I kept near him, absorbed in studying him in silence.

Louis Lambert was slightly built, nearly five feet in height; his face was tanned, and his hands were burnt brown by the sun, giving him an appearance of manly vigor, which, in fact, he did not possess. Indeed, two months after he came to the college, when studying in the classroom had faded his vivid, so to speak, vegetable coloring, he became as pale and white as a woman.

His head was unusually large. His hair, of a fine, bright black in masses of curls, gave wonderful beauty to his brow, of which the proportions were extraordinary even to us heedless boys, knowing nothing, as may be supposed, of the auguries of phrenology, a science still in its cradle. The distinction of this prophetic brow lay principally in the exquisitely chiseled shape of the arches under which his black eyes sparkled, and which had the transparency of alabaster, the line having the unusual beauty of being perfectly level to where it met the top of the nose. But when you saw his eyes it was difficult to think of the rest of his face, which was indeed plain enough, for their look was full of a wonderful variety of expression; they seemed to have a soul in their depths. At one moment astonishingly clear and piercing, at another full of heavenly sweetness, those eyes became dull, almost colorless, as it seemed, when he was lost in meditation. They then looked like a window from which the sun had suddenly vanished after lighting it up. His strength and his voice were no less variable; equally rigid, equally unexpected. His tone could be as sweet as that of a woman compelled to own her love; at other times it was labored, rough, rugged, if I may use such words in a new sense. As to his strength, he was habitually incapable of enduring the fatigue of any game, and seemed weakly, almost infirm. But during the early days of his school-life, one of our little bullies having made game of this sickliness, which rendered him unfit for the violent exercise in vogue among his fellows, Lambert took hold with both hands of one of the class-tables, consisting of twelve large desks, face to face and sloping from the middle; he leaned back against the class-master's desk, steadying the table with his feet on the cross-bar below, and said:

"Now, ten of you try to move it!"

I was present, and can vouch for this strange display of strength; it was impossible to move the table.

Lambert had the gift of summoning to his aid at certain times the most extraordinary powers, and of concentrating all his forces on a given point. But children, like men, are wont to judge of everything by first impressions, and after the first few days we ceased to study Louis; he entirely belied Madame de Stael's prognostications, and displayed none of the prodigies we looked for in him.

After three months at school, Louis was looked upon as a quite ordinary scholar. I alone was allowed really to know that sublime—why should I not say divine?—soul, for what is nearer to God than genius in the heart of a child? The similarity of our tastes and ideas made us friends and chums; our intimacy was so brotherly that our school-fellows joined our two names; one was never spoken without the other, and to call either they always shouted "Poet-and-Pythagoras!" Some other names had been known coupled in a like manner. Thus for two years I was the school friend of poor Louis Lambert; and during that time my life was so identified with his, that I am enabled now to write his intellectual biography.

It was long before I fully knew the poetry and the wealth of ideas that lay hidden in my companion's heart and brain. It was not till I was thirty years of age, till my experience was matured and condensed, till the flash of an intense illumination had thrown a fresh light upon it, that I was capable of understanding all the bearings of the phenomena which I witnessed at that early time. I benefited by them without understanding their greatness or their processes; indeed, I have forgotten some, or remember only the most conspicuous facts; still, my memory is now able to co-ordinate them, and I have mastered the secrets of that fertile brain by looking back to the delightful days of our boyish affection. So it was time alone that initiated me into the meaning of the events and facts that were crowded into that obscure life, as into that of many another man who is lost to science. Indeed, this narrative, so far as the expression and appreciation of many things is concerned, will be found full of what may be termed moral anachronisms, which perhaps will not detract from its peculiar interest.

In the course of the first few months after coming to Vendome, Louis became the victim of a malady which, though the symptoms were invisible to the eye of our superiors, considerably interfered with the exercise of his remarkable gifts. Accustomed to live in the open air, and to the freedom of a purely haphazard education, happy in the tender care of an old man who was devoted to him, used to meditating in the sunshine, he found it very hard to submit to college rules, to walk in the ranks, to live within the four walls of a room where eighty boys were sitting in silence on wooden forms each in front of his desk. His senses were developed to such perfection as gave them the most sensitive keenness, and every part of him suffered from this life in common.

The effluvia that vitiated the air, mingled with the odors of a classroom that was never clean, nor free from the fragments of our breakfasts or snacks, affected his sense of smell, the sense which, being more immediately connected than the others with the nerve-centers of the brain, must, when shocked, cause invisible disturbance to the organs of thought.

Besides these elements of impurity in the atmosphere, there were lockers in the classrooms in which the boys kept their miscellaneous plunder—pigeons killed for fete days, or tidbits filched from the dinner-table. In each classroom, too, there was a large stone slab, on which two pails full of water were kept standing, a sort of sink, where we every morning washed our faces and hands, one after another, in the master's presence. We then passed on to a table, where women combed and powdered our hair. Thus the place, being cleaned but once a day before we were up, was always more or less dirty. In spite of numerous windows and lofty doors, the air was constantly fouled by the smells from the washing-place, the hairdressing, the lockers, and the thousand messes made by the boys, to say nothing of their eighty closely packed bodies. And this sort of humus, mingling with the mud we brought in from the playing-yard, produced a suffocatingly pestilent muck-heap.

The loss of the fresh and fragrant country air in which he had hitherto lived, the change of habits and strict discipline, combined to depress Lambert. With his elbow on his desk and his head supported on his left hand, he spent the hours of study gazing at the trees in the court or the clouds in the sky; he seemed to be thinking of his lessons; but the master, seeing his pen motionless, or the sheet before him still a blank, would call out:

"Lambert, you are doing nothing!"

This "you are doing nothing!" was a pin-thrust that wounded Louis to the quick. And then he never earned the rest of the play-time; he always had impositions to write. The imposition, a punishment which varies according to the practice of different schools, consisted at Vendome of a certain number of lines to be written out in play hours. Lambert and I were so overpowered with impositions, that we had not six free days during the two years of our school friendship. But for the books we took out of the library, which maintained some vitality in our brains, this system of discipline would have reduced us to idiotcy. Want of exercise is fatal to children. The habit of preserving a dignified appearance, begun in tender infancy, has, it is said, a visible effect on the constitution of royal personages when the faults of such an education are not counteracted by the life of the battle-field or the laborious sport of hunting. And if the laws of etiquette and Court manners can act on the spinal marrow to such an extent as to affect the pelvis of kings, to soften their cerebral tissue, and so degenerate the race, what deep-seated mischief, physical and moral, must result in schoolboys from the constant lack of air, exercise, and cheerfulness!

Indeed, the rules of punishment carried out in schools deserve the attention of the Office of Public Instruction when any thinkers are to be found there who do not think exclusively of themselves.

We incurred the infliction of an imposition in a thousand ways. Our memory was so good that we never learned a lesson. It was enough for either of us to hear our class-fellows repeat the task in French, Latin, or grammar, and we could say it when our turn came; but if the master, unfortunately, took it into his head to reverse the usual order and call upon us first, we very often did not even know what the lesson was; then the imposition fell in spite of our most ingenious excuses. Then we always put off writing our exercises till the last moment; if there were a book to be finished, or if we were lost in thought, the task was forgotten—again an imposition. How often have we scribbled an exercise during the time when the head-boy, whose business it was to collect them when we came into school, was gathering them from the others!

In addition to the moral misery which Lambert went through in trying to acclimatize himself to college life, there was a scarcely less cruel apprenticeship through which every boy had to pass: to those bodily sufferings which seemed infinitely varied. The tenderness of a child's skin needs extreme care, especially in winter, when a school-boy is constantly exchanging the frozen air of the muddy playing-yard for the stuffy atmosphere of the classroom. The "little boys" and the smallest of all, for lack of a mother's care, were martyrs to chilblains and chaps so severe that they had to be regularly dressed during the breakfast hour; but this could only be very indifferently done to so many damaged hands, toes, and heels. A good many of the boys indeed were obliged to prefer the evil to the remedy; the choice constantly lay between their lessons waiting to be finished or the joys of a slide, and waiting for a bandage carelessly put on, and still more carelessly cast off again. Also it was the fashion in the school to gibe at the poor, feeble creatures who went to be doctored; the bullies vied with each other in snatching off the rags which the infirmary nurse had tied on. Hence, in winter, many of us, with half-dead feet and fingers, sick with pain, were incapable of work, and punished for not working. The Fathers, too often deluded by shammed ailments, would not believe in real suffering.

The price paid for our schooling and board also covered the cost of clothing. The committee contracted for the shoes and clothes supplied to the boys; hence the weekly inspection of which I have spoken. This plan, though admirable for the manager, is always disastrous to the managed. Woe to the boy who indulged in the bad habit of treading his shoes down at heel, of cracking the shoe-leather, or wearing out the soles too fast, whether from a defect in his gait, or by fidgeting during lessons in obedience to the instinctive need of movement common to all children. That boy did not get through the winter without great suffering. In the first place, his chilblains would ache and shot as badly as a fit of the gout; then the rivets and pack-thread intended to repair the shoes would give way, or the broken heels would prevent the wretched shoes from keeping on his feet; he was obliged to drag them wearily along the frozen roads, or sometimes to dispute their possession with the clay soil of the district; the water and snow got in through some unnoticed crack or ill-sewn patch, and the foot would swell.

Out of sixty boys, not ten perhaps could walk without some special form of torture; and yet they all kept up with the body of the troop, dragged on by the general movement, as men are driven through life by life itself. Many a time some proud-tempered boy would shed tears of rage while summoning his remaining energy to run ahead and get home again in spite of pain, so sensitively afraid of laughter or of pity—two forms of scorn—is the still tender soul at that age.

At school, as in social life, the strong despise the feeble without knowing in what true strength consists.

Nor was this all. No gloves. If by good hap a boy's parents, the infirmary nurse, or the headmaster gave gloves to a particularly delicate lad, the wags or the big boys of the class would put them on the stove, amused to see them dry and shrivel; or if the gloves escaped the marauders, after getting wet they shrunk as they dried for want of care. No, gloves were impossible. Gloves were a privilege, and boys insist on equality.

Louis Lambert fell a victim to all these varieties of torment. Like many contemplative men, who, when lost in thought, acquire a habit of mechanical motion, he had a mania for fidgeting with his shoes, and destroyed them very quickly. His girlish complexion, the skin of his ears and lips, cracked with the least cold. His soft, white hands grew red and swollen. He had perpetual colds. Thus he was a constant sufferer till he became inured to school-life. Taught at last by cruel experience, he was obliged to "look after his things," to use the school phrase. He was forced to take care of his locker, his desk, his clothes, his shoes; to protect his ink, his books, his copy-paper, and his pens from pilferers; in short, to give his mind to the thousand details of our trivial life, to which more selfish and commonplace minds devoted such strict attention—thus infallibly securing prizes for "proficiency" and "good conduct"—while they were overlooked by a boy of the highest promise, who, under the hand of an almost divine imagination, gave himself up with rapture to the flow of his ideas.

This was not all. There is a perpetual struggle going on

between the masters and the boys, a struggle without truce, to be compared with nothing else in the social world, unless it be the resistance of the opposition to the ministry in a representative government. But journalists and opposition speakers are probably less prompt to take advantage of a weak point, less extreme in resenting an injury, and less merciless in their mockery than boys are in regard to those who rule over them. It is a task to put angels out of patience. An unhappy class-master must then not be too severely blamed, ill-paid as he is, and consequently not too competent, if he is occasionally unjust or out of temper. Perpetually watched by a hundred mocking eyes, and surrounded with snares, he sometimes revenges himself for his own blunders on the boys who are only too ready to detect them.

Unless for serious misdemeanors, for which there were other forms of punishment, the strap was regarded at Vendome as the ultima ratio Patrum. Exercises forgotten, lessons ill learned, common ill behavior were sufficiently punished by an imposition, but offended dignity spoke in the master through the strap. Of all the physical torments to which we were exposed, certainly the most acute was that inflicted by this leathern instrument, about two fingers wide, applied to our poor little hands with all the strength and all the fury of the administrator. To endure this classical form of correction, the victim knelt in the middle of the room. He had to leave his form and go to kneel down near the master's desk under the curious and generally merciless eyes of his fellows. To sensitive natures these preliminaries were an introductory torture, like the journey from the Palais de Justice to the Place de Greve which the condemned used to make to the scaffold.

Some boys cried out and shed bitter tears before or after the application of the strap; others accepted the infliction with stoic calm; it was a question of nature; but few could control an expression of anguish in anticipation.

Louis Lambert was constantly enduring the strap, and owed it to a peculiarity of his physiognomy of which he was for a long time quite unconscious. Whenever he was suddenly roused from a fit of abstraction by the master's cry, "You are doing nothing!" it often happened that, without knowing it, he flashed at his teacher a look full of fierce contempt, and charged with thought, as a Leyden jar is charged with electricity. This look, no doubt, discomfited the master, who, indignant at this unspoken retort, wished to cure his scholar of that thunderous flash.

The first time the Father took offence at this ray of scorn, which struck him like a lightning-flash, he made this speech, as I well remember:

"If you look at me again in that way, Lambert, you will get the strap."

At these words every nose was in the air, every eye looked alternately at the master and at Louis. The observation was so utterly foolish, that the boy again looked at the Father, overwhelming him with another flash. From this arose a standing feud between Lambert and his master, resulting in a certain amount of "strap." Thus did he first discover the power of his eye.

The hapless poet, so full of nerves, as sensitive as a woman, under the sway of chronic melancholy, and as sick with genius as a girl with love that she pines for, knowing nothing of it;—this boy, at once so powerful and so weak, transplanted by "Corinne" from the country he loved, to be squeezed in the mould of a collegiate routine to which every spirit and every body must yield, whatever their range or temperament, accepting its rule and its uniform as gold is crushed into round coin under the press; Louis Lambert suffered in every spot where pain can touch the soul or the flesh. Stuck on a form, restricted to the acreage of his desk, a victim of the strap and to a sickly frame, tortured in every sense, environed by distress—everything compelled him to give his body up to the myriad tyrannies of school life; and, like the martyrs who smiled in the midst of suffering, he took refuge in heaven, which lay open to his mind. Perhaps this life of purely inward emotions helped him to see something of the mysteries he so entirely believed in!

Our independence, our illicit amusements, our apparent waste of time, our persistent indifference, our frequent punishments and aversion for our exercises and impositions, earned us a reputation, which no one cared to controvert, for being an idle and incorrigible pair. Our masters treated us with contempt, and we fell into utter disgrace with our companions, from whom we concealed our secret studies for fear of being laughed at. This hard judgment, which was injustice in the masters, was but natural in our schoolfellows. We could neither play ball, nor run races, nor walk on stilts. On exceptional holidays, when amnesty was proclaimed and we got a few hours of freedom, we shared in none of the popular diversions of the school. Aliens from the pleasures enjoyed by the others, we were outcasts, sitting forlorn under a tree in the playing-ground. The Poet-and-Pythagoras formed an exception and led a life apart from the life of the rest.

The penetrating instinct and unerring conceit of schoolboys made them feel that we were of a nature either far above or far beneath their own; hence some simply hated our aristocratic reserve, others merely scorned our ineptitude. These feelings were equally shared by us without our knowing it; perhaps I have but now divined them. We lived exactly like two rats, huddled into the corner of the room where our desks were, sitting there alike during lesson time and play hours. This strange state of affairs inevitably and in fact placed us on a footing of war with all the other boys in our division. Forgotten for the most part, we sat there very contentedly; half happy, like two plants, two images who would have been missed from the furniture of the room. But the most aggressive of our schoolfellows would sometimes torment us, just to show their malignant power, and we responded with stolid contempt, which brought many a thrashing down on the Poet-and-Pythagoras.

Lambert's home-sickness lasted for many months. I know no words to describe the dejection to which he was a prey. Louis has taken the glory off many a masterpiece for me. We had both played the part of the "Leper of Aosta," and had both experienced the feelings described in Monsieur de Maistre's story, before we read them as expressed by his eloquent pen. A book may, indeed, revive the memories of our childhood, but it can never compete with them successfully. Lambert's woes had taught me many a chant of sorrow far more appealing than the finest passages in "Werther." And, indeed, there is no possible comparison between the pangs of a passion condemned, whether rightly or wrongly, by every law, and the grief of a poor child pining for the glorious sunshine, the dews of the valley, and liberty. Werther is the slave of desire; Louis Lambert was an enslaved soul. Given equal talent, the more pathetic sorrow, founded on desires which, being purer, are the more genuine, must transcend the wail even of genius.

After sitting for a long time with his eyes fixed on a lime-tree in the playground, Louis would say just a word; but that word would reveal an infinite speculation.

"Happily for me," he exclaimed one day, "there are hours of comfort when I feel as though the walls of the room had fallen and I were away—away in the fields! What a pleasure it is to let oneself go on the stream of one's thoughts as a bird is borne up on its wings!"

"Why is green a color so largely diffused throughout creation?" he would ask me. "Why are there so few straight lines in nature? Why is it that man, in his structures, rarely introduces curves? Why is it that he alone, of all creatures, has a sense of straightness?"

These queries revealed long excursions in space. He had, I am sure, seen vast landscapes, fragrant with the scent of woods. He was always silent and resigned, a living elegy, always suffering but unable to complain of suffering. An eagle that needed the world to feed him, shut in between four narrow, dirty walls; and thus this life became an ideal life in the strictest meaning of the words. Filled as he was with contempt of the almost useless studies to which we were harnessed, Louis went on his skyward way absolutely unconscious of the things about us.

I, obeying the imitative instinct that is so strong in childhood, tired to regulate my life in conformity with his. And Louis the more easily infected me with the sort of torpor in which deep contemplation leaves the body, because I was younger and more impressionable than he. Like two lovers, we got into the habit of thinking together in a common reverie. His intuitions had already acquired that acuteness which must surely characterize the intellectual perceptiveness of great poets and often bring them to the verge of madness.

"Do you ever feel," said he to me one day, "as though imagined suffering affected you in spite of yourself? If, for instance, I think with concentration of the effect that the blade of my penknife would have in piercing my flesh, I feel an acute pain as if I had really cut myself; only the blood is wanting. But the pain comes suddenly, and startles me like a sharp noise breaking profound silence. Can an idea cause physical pain?—What do you say to that, eh?"

When he gave utterance to such subtle reflections, we both fell into artless meditation; we set to work to detect in ourselves the inscrutable phenomena of the origin of thoughts, which Lambert hoped to discover in their earliest germ, so as to describe some day the unknown process. Then, after much discussion, often mixed up with childish notions, a look would flash from Lambert's eager eyes; he would grasp my hand, and a word from the depths of his soul would show the current of his mind.

"Thinking is seeing," said he one day, carried away by some objection raised as to the first principles of our organization. "Every human science is based on deduction, which is a slow process of seeing by which we work up from the effect to the cause; or, in a wider sense, all poetry, like every work of art, proceeds from a swift vision of things."

He was a spiritualist (as opposed to materialism); but I would venture to contradict him, using his own arguments to consider the intellect as a purely physical phenomenon. We both were right. Perhaps the words materialism and spiritualism express the two faces of the same fact. His considerations on the substance of the mind led to his accepting, with a certain pride, the life of privation to which we were condemned in consequence of our idleness and our indifference to learning. He had a certain consciousness of his own powers which bore him up through his spiritual cogitations. How delightful it was to me to feel his soul acting on my own! Many a time have we remained sitting on our form, both buried in one book, having quite forgotten each other's existence, and yet not apart; each conscious of the other's presence, and bathing in an ocean of thought, like two fish swimming in the same waters.

Our life, apparently, was merely vegetating; but we lived through our heart and brain.

Lambert's influence over my imagination left traces that still abide. I used to listen hungrily to his tales, full of the marvels which make men, as well as children, rapturously devour stories in which truth assumes the most grotesque forms. His passion for mystery, and the credulity natural to the young, often led us to discuss Heaven and Hell. Then Louis, by expounding Swedenborg, would try to make me share in his beliefs concerning angels. In his least logical arguments there were still amazing observations as to the powers of man, which gave his words that color of truth without which nothing can be done in any art. The romantic end he foresaw as the destiny of man was calculated to flatter the yearning which tempts blameless imaginations to give themselves up to beliefs. Is it not during the youth of a nation that its dogmas and idols are conceived? And are not the supernatural beings before whom the people tremble the personification of their feelings and their magnified desires?

All that I can now remember of the poetical conversations we held together concerning the Swedish prophet, whose works I have since had the curiosity to read, may be told in a few paragraphs.

In each of us there are two distinct beings. According to Swedenborg, the angel is an individual in whom the inner being conquers the external being. If a man desires to earn his call to be an angel, as soon as his mind reveals to him his twofold existence, he must strive to foster the delicate angelic essence that exists within him. If, for lack of a lucid appreciation of his destiny, he allows bodily action to predominate, instead of confirming his intellectual being, all his powers will be absorbed in the use of his external senses, and the angel will slowly perish by the materialization of both natures. In the contrary case, if he nourishes his inner being with the aliment needful to it, the soul triumphs over matter and strives to get free.

When they separate by the act of what we call death, the angel, strong enough then to cast off its wrappings, survives and begins its real life. The infinite variety which differentiates individual men can only be explained by this twofold existence, which, again, is proved and made intelligible by that variety.

In point of fact, the wide distance between a man whose torpid intelligence condemns him to evident stupidity, and one who, by the exercise of his inner life, has acquired the gift of some power, allows us to suppose that there is as great a difference between men of genius and other beings as there is between the blind and those who see. This hypothesis, since it extends creation beyond all limits, gives us, as it were, the clue to heaven. The beings who, here on earth, are apparently mingled without distinction, are there distributed, according to their inner perfection, in distinct spheres whose speech and manners have nothing in common. In the invisible world, as in the real world, if some native of the lower spheres comes, all unworthy, into a higher sphere, not only can he never understand the customs and language there, but his mere presence paralyzes the voice and hearts of those who dwell therein.

Dante, in his Divine Comedy, had perhaps some slight intuition of those spheres which begin in the world of torment, and rise, circle on circle, to the highest heaven. Thus Swedenborg's doctrine is the product of a lucid spirit noting down the innumerable signs by which the angels manifest their presence among men.

This doctrine, which I have endeavored to sum up in a more or less consistent form, was set before me by Lambert with all the fascination of mysticism, swathed in the wrappings of the phraseology affected by mystical writers: an obscure language full of abstractions, and taking such effect on the brain, that there are books by Jacob Boehm, Swedenborg, and Madame Guyon, so strangely powerful that they give rise to phantasies as various as the dreams of the opium-eater. Lambert told me of mystical facts so extraordinary, he so acted on my imagination, that he made my brain reel. Still, I loved to plunge into that realm of mystery, invisible to the senses, in which every one likes to dwell, whether he pictures it to himself under the indefinite ideal of the Future, or clothes it in the more solid guise of romance. These violent revulsions of the mind on itself gave me, without my knowing it, a comprehension of its power, and accustomed me to the workings of the mind.

Lambert himself explained everything by his theory of the angels. To him pure love—love as we dream of it in youth—was the coalescence of two angelic natures. Nothing could exceed the fervency with which he longed to meet a woman angel. And who better than he could inspire or feel love? If anything could give an impression of an exquisite nature, was it not the amiability and kindliness that marked his feelings, his words, his actions, his slightest gestures, the conjugal regard that united us as boys, and that we expressed when we called ourselves chums?

There was no distinction for us between my ideas and his. We imitated each other's handwriting, so that one might write the tasks of both. Thus, if one of us had a book to finish and to return to the mathematical master, he could read on without interruption while the other scribbled off his exercise and imposition. We did our tasks as though paying a task on our peace of mind. If my memory does not play me false, they were sometimes of remarkable merit when Lambert did them. But on the foregone conclusion that we were both of us idiots, the master always went through them under a rooted prejudice, and even kept them to read to be laughed at by our schoolfellows.

I remember one afternoon, at the end of the lesson, which lasted from two till four, the master took possession of a page of translation by Lambert. The passage began with Caius Gracchus, vir nobilis; Lambert had construed this by "Caius Gracchus had a noble heart."

"Where do you find 'heart' in nobilis?" said the Father sharply.

And there was a roar of laughter, while Lambert looked at the master in some bewilderment.

"What would Madame la Baronne de Stael say if she could know that you make such nonsense of a word that means noble family, of patrician rank?"

"She would say that you were an ass!" said I in a muttered tone.

"Master Poet, you will stay in for a week," replied the master, who unfortunately overheard me.

Lambert simply repeated, looking at me with inexpressible affection, "Vir nobilis!"

Madame de Stael was, in fact, partly the cause of Lambert's troubles. On every pretext masters and pupils threw the name in his teeth, either in irony or in reproof.

Louis lost no time in getting himself "kept in" to share my

imprisonment. Freer thus than in any other circumstances, we could talk the whole day long in the silence of the dormitories, where each boy had a cubicle six feet square, the partitions consisting at the top of open bars. The doors, fitted with gratings, were locked at night and opened in the morning under the eye of the Father whose duty it was to superintend our rising and going to bed. The creak of these gates, which the college servants unlocked with remarkable expedition, was a sound peculiar to that college. These little cells were our prison, and boys were sometimes shut up there for a month at a time. The boys in these coops were under the stern eye of the prefect, a sort of censor who stole up at certain hours, or at unexpected moments, with a silent step, to hear if we were talking instead of writing our impositions. But a few walnut shells dropped on the stairs, or the sharpness of our hearing, almost always enabled us to beware of his coming, so we could give ourselves up without anxiety to our favorite studies. However, as books were prohibited, our prison hours were chiefly filled up with metaphysical discussions, or with relating singular facts connected with the phenomena of mind.

One of the most extraordinary of these incidents beyond question is this, which I will here record, not only because it concerns Lambert, but because it perhaps was the turning-point of his scientific career. By the law of custom in all schools, Thursday and Sunday were holidays; but the services, which we were made to attend very regularly, so completely filled up Sunday, that we considered Thursday our only real day of freedom. After once attending Mass, we had a long day before us to spend in walks in the country round the town of Vendome. The manor of Rochambeau was the most interesting object of our excursions, perhaps by reason of its distance; the smaller boys were very seldom taken on so fatiguing an expedition. However, once or twice a year the class-masters would hold out Rochambeau as a reward for diligence.

In 1812, towards the end of the spring, we were to go there for the first time. Our anxiety to see this famous chateau of Rochambeau, where the owner sometimes treated the boys to milk, made us all very good, and nothing hindered the outing. Neither

Lambert nor I had ever seen the pretty valley of the Loire where the house stood. So his imagination and mine were much excited by the prospect of this excursion, which filled the school with traditional glee. We talked of it all the evening, planning to spend in fruit or milk such money as we had saved, against all the habits of school-life.

After dinner next day, we set out at half-past twelve, each provided with a square hunch of bread, given to us for our afternoon snack. And off we went, as gay as swallows, marching in a body on the famous chateau with an eagerness which would at first allow of no fatigue. When we reached the hill, whence we looked down on the house standing half-way down the slope, on the devious valley through which the river winds and sparkles between meadows in graceful curves—a beautiful landscape, one of those scenes to which the keen emotions of early youth or of love lend such a charm, that it is wise never to see them again in later years—Louis Lambert said to me, "Why, I saw this last night in a dream."

He recognized the clump of trees under which we were standing, the grouping of the woods, the color of the water, the turrets of the chateau, the details, the distance, in fact every part of the prospect which we looked on for the first time. We were mere children; I, at any rate, who was but thirteen; Louis, at fifteen, might have the precocity of genius, but at that time we were incapable of falsehood in the most trivial matters of our life as friends. Indeed, if Lambert's powerful mind had any presentiment of the importance of such facts, he was far from appreciating their whole bearing; and he was quite astonished by this incident. I asked him if he had not perhaps been brought to Rochambeau in his infancy, and my question struck him; but after thinking it over, he answered in the negative. This incident, analogous to what may be known of the phenomena of sleep in several persons, will illustrate the beginnings of Lambert's line of talent; he took it, in fact, as the basis of a whole system, using a fragment—as Cuvier did in another branch of inquiry—as a clue to the reconstruction of a complete system.

At this moment we were sitting together on an old oak-stump, and after a few minutes' reflection, Louis said to me:

"If the landscape did not come to me—which it is absurd to imagine—I must have come here. If I was here while I was asleep in my cubicle, does not that constitute a complete severance of my body and my inner being? Does it not prove some inscrutable locomotive faculty in the spirit with effects resembling those of locomotion in the body? Well, then, if my spirit and my body can be severed during sleep, why should I not insist on their separating in the same way while I am awake? I see no half-way mean between the two propositions.

"But if we go further into details: either the facts are due to the action of a faculty which brings out a second being to whom my body is merely a husk, since I was in my cell, and yet I saw the landscape—and this upsets many systems; or the facts took place either in some nerve centre, of which the name is yet to be discovered, where our feelings dwell and move; or else in the cerebral centre, where ideas are formed. This last hypothesis gives rise to some strange questions. I walked, I saw, I heard. Motion is inconceivable but in space, sound acts only at certain angles or on surfaces, color is caused only by light. If, in the dark, with my eyes shut, I saw, in myself, colored objects; if I heard sounds in the most perfect silence and without the conditions requisite for the production of sound; if without stirring I traversed wide tracts of space, there must be inner faculties independent of the external laws of physics. Material nature must be penetrable by the spirit.

"How is it that men have hitherto given so little thought to the phenomena of sleep, which seem to prove that man has a double life? May there not be a new science lying beneath them?" he added, striking his brow with his hand. "If not the elements of a science, at any rate the revelation of stupendous powers in man; at least they prove a frequent severance of our two natures, the fact I have been thinking out for a very long time. At last, then, I have hit on evidence to show the superiority that distinguishes our latent senses from our corporeal senses! Homo duplex!

"And yet," he went on, after a pause, with a doubtful shrug, "perhaps we have not two natures; perhaps we are merely gifted with personal and perfectible qualities, of which the development within us produces certain unobserved phenomena of activity, penetration, and vision. In our love of the marvelous, a passion begotten of our pride, we have translated these effects into poetical inventions, because we did not understand them. It is so convenient to deify the incomprehensible!

"I should, I own, lament over the loss of my illusions. I so much wished to believe in our twofold nature and in Swedenborg's angels. Must this new science destroy them? Yes; for the study of our unknown properties involves us in a science that appears to be materialistic, for the Spirit uses, divides, and animates the Substance; but it does not destroy it."

He remained pensive, almost sad. Perhaps he saw the dreams of his youth as swaddling clothes that he must soon shake off.

"Sight and hearing are, no doubt, the sheaths for a very marvelous instrument," said he, laughing at his own figure of speech.

Always when he was talking to me of Heaven and Hell, he was wont to treat of Nature as being master; but now, as he pronounced these last words, big with prescience, he seemed to soar more boldly than ever above the landscape, and his forehead seemed ready to burst with the afflatus of genius. His powers—mental powers we must call them till some new term is found—seemed to flash from the organs intended to express them. His eyes shot out thoughts; his uplifted hand, his silent but tremulous lips were eloquent; his burning glance was radiant; at last his head, as though too heavy, or exhausted by too eager a flight, fell on his breast. This boy—this giant—bent his head, took my hand and clasped it in his own, which was damp, so fevered was he for the search for truth; then, after a pause, he said:

"I shall be famous!—And you, too," he added after a pause. "We will both study the Chemistry of the Will."

Noble soul! I recognized his superiority, though he took great care never to make me feel it. He shared with me all the treasures of his mind, and regarded me as instrumental in his discoveries, leaving me the credit of my insignificant contributions. He was always as gracious as a woman in love; he had all the bashful feeling, the delicacy of soul which make life happy and pleasant to endure.

On the following day he began writing what he called a Treatise on the Will; his subsequent reflections led to many changes in its plan and method; but the incident of that day was certainly the germ of the work, just as the electric shock always felt by Mesmer at the approach of a particular manservant was the starting-point of his discoveries in magnetism, a science till then interred under the mysteries of Isis, of Delphi, of the cave of Trophonius, and rediscovered by that prodigious genius, close on Lavater, and the precursor of Gall.

Lambert's ideas, suddenly illuminated by this flash of light, assumed vaster proportions; he disentangled certain truths from his many acquisitions and brought them into order; then, like a founder, he cast the model of his work. At the end of six months' indefatigable labor, Lambert's writings excited the curiosity of our companions, and became the object of cruel practical jokes which led to a fatal issue.

One day one of the masters, who was bent on seeing the manuscripts, enlisted the aid of our tyrants, and came to seize, by force, a box that contained the precious papers. Lambert and I defended it with incredible courage. The trunk was locked, our aggressors could not open it, but they tried to smash it in the struggle, a stroke of malignity at which we shrieked with rage. Some of the boys, with a sense of justice, or struck perhaps by our heroic defence, advised the attacking party to leave us in peace, crushing us with insulting contempt. But suddenly, brought to the spot by the noise of a battle, Father Haugoult roughly intervened, inquiring as to the cause of the fight. Our enemies had interrupted us in writing our impositions, and the class-master came to protect his slaves. The foe, in self-defence, betrayed the existence of the manuscript. The dreadful Haugoult insisted on our giving up the box; if we should resist, he would have it broken open. Lambert gave him the key; the master took out the papers, glanced through them, and said, as he confiscated them:

"And it is for such rubbish as this that you neglect your lessons!"

Large tears fell from Lambert's eyes, wrung from him as much by a sense of his offended moral superiority as by the gratuitous insult and betrayal that he had suffered. We gave the accusers a glance of stern reproach: had they not delivered us over to the common enemy? If the common law of school entitled them to thrash us, did it not require them to keep silence as to our misdeeds?

In a moment they were no doubt ashamed of their baseness.

Father Haugoult probably sold the Treatise on the Will to a local grocer, unconscious of the scientific treasure, of which the germs thus fell into unworthy hands.

Six months later I left the school, and I do not know whether Lambert ever recommenced his labors. Our parting threw him into a mood of the darkest melancholy.

It was in memory of the disaster that befell Louis' book that, in the tale which comes first in these Etudes, I adopted the title invented by Lambert for a work of fiction, and gave the name of a woman who was dear to him to a girl characterized by her self-devotion; but this is not all I have borrowed from him: his character and occupations were of great value to me in writing that book, and the subject arose from some reminiscences of our youthful meditations. This present volume is intended as a modest monument, a broken column, to commemorate the life of the man who bequeathed to me all he had to leave—his thoughts.

In that boyish effort Lambert had enshrined the ideas of a man. Ten years later, when I met some learned men who were devoting serious attention to the phenomena that had struck us and that Lambert had so marvelously analyzed, I understood the value of his work, then already forgotten as childish. I at once spent several months in recalling the principal theories discovered by my poor schoolmate. Having collected my reminiscences, I can boldly state that, by 1812, he had proved, divined, and set forth in his Treatise several important facts of which, as he had declared, evidence was certain to come sooner or later. His philosophical speculations ought undoubtedly to gain him recognition as one of the great thinkers who have appeared at wide intervals among men, to reveal to them the bare skeleton of some science to come, of which the roots spread slowly, but which, in due time, bring forth fair fruit in the intellectual sphere. Thus a humble artisan, Bernard Palissy, searching the soil to find minerals for glazing pottery, proclaimed, in the sixteenth century, with the infallible intuition of genius, geological facts which it is now the glory of Cuvier and Buffon to have demonstrated.

I can, I believe, give some idea of Lambert's Treatise by stating the chief propositions on which it was based; but, in spite of myself, I shall strip them of the ideas in which they were clothed, and which were indeed their indispensable accompaniment. I started on a different path, and only made use of those of his researches which answered the purpose of my scheme. I know not, therefore, whether as his disciple I can faithfully expound his views, having assimilated them in the first instance so as to color them with my own.

New ideas require new words, or a new and expanded use of old words, extended and defined in their meaning. Thus Lambert, to set forth the basis of his system, had adopted certain common words that answered to his notions. The word Will he used to connote the medium in which the mind moves, or to use a less abstract expression, the mass of power by which man can reproduce, outside himself, the actions constituting his external life. Volition—a word due to Locke—expressed the act by which a man exerts his will. The word Mind, or Thought, which he regarded as the quintessential product of the Will, also represented the medium in which the ideas originate to which thought gives substance. The Idea, a name common to every creation of the brain, constituted the act by which man uses his mind. Thus the Will and the Mind were the two generating forces; the Volition and the Idea were the two products. Volition, he thought, was the Idea evolved from the abstract state to a concrete state, from its generative fluid to a solid expression, so to speak, if such words may be taken to formulate notions so difficult of definition. According to him, the Mind and Ideas are the motion and the outcome of our inner organization, just as the Will and Volition are of our external activity.

He gave the Will precedence over the Mind.

"You must will before you can think," he said. "Many beings

live in a condition of Willing without ever attaining to the condition of Thinking. In the North, life is long; in the South, it is shorter; but in the North we see torpor, in the South a constant excitability of the Will, up to the point where from an excess of cold or of heat the organs are almost nullified."

The use of the word "medium" was suggested to him by an observation he had made in his childhood, though, to be sure, he had no suspicion then of its importance, but its singularity naturally struck his delicately alert imagination. His mother, a fragile, nervous woman, all sensitiveness and affection, was one of those beings created to represent womanhood in all the perfection of her attributes, but relegated by a mistaken fate to too low a place in the social scale. Wholly loving, and consequently wholly suffering, she died young, having thrown all her energies into her motherly love. Lambert, a child of six, lying, but not always sleeping, in a cot by his mother's bed, saw the electric sparks from her hair when she combed it. The man of fifteen made scientific application of this fact which had amused the child, a fact beyond dispute, of which there is ample evidence in many instances, especially of women who by a sad fatality are doomed to let unappreciated feelings evaporate in the air, or some superabundant power run to waste.

In support of his definitions, Lambert propounded a variety of problems to be solved, challenges flung out to science, though he proposed to seek the solution for himself. He inquired, for instance, whether the element that constitutes electricity does not enter as a base into the specific fluid whence our Ideas and Volitions proceed? Whether the hair, which loses its color, turns white, falls out, or disappears, in proportion to the decay or crystallization of our thoughts, may not be in fact a capillary system, either absorbent or diffusive, and wholly electrical? Whether the fluid phenomena of the Will, a matter generated within us, and spontaneously reacting under the impress of conditions as yet unobserved, were at all more extraordinary than those of the invisible and intangible fluid produced by a voltaic pile, and applied to the nervous system of a dead man? Whether the formation of Ideas and their constant diffusion was less incomprehensible than evaporation of the atoms, imperceptible indeed, but so violent in their effects, that are given off from a grain of musk without any loss of weight. Whether, granting that the function of the skin is purely protective, absorbent, excretive, and tactile, the circulation of the blood and all its mechanism would not correspond with the transsubstantiation of our Will, as the circulation of the nerve fluid corresponds to that of the Mind? Finally, whether the more or less rapid affluence of these two real substances may not be the result of a certain perfection or imperfection of organs whose conditions require investigation in every manifestation?

Having set forth these principles, he proposed to class the phenomena of human life in two series of distinct results, demanding, with the ardent insistency of conviction, a special analysis for each. In fact, having observed in almost every type of created thing two separate motions, he assumed, nay, he asserted, their existence in our human nature, and designated this vital antithesis Action and Reaction.

"A desire," he said, "is a fact completely accomplished in our will before it is accomplished externally."

Hence the sum-total of our Volitions and our Ideas constitutes Action, and the sum-total of our external acts he called Reaction.

When I subsequently read the observations made by Bichat on the duality of our external senses, I was really bewildered by my recollections, recognizing the startling coincidences between the views of that celebrated physiologist and those of Louis Lambert. They both died young, and they had with equal steps arrived at the same strange truths. Nature has in every case been pleased to give a twofold purpose to the various apparatus that constitute her creatures; and the twofold action of the human organism, which is now ascertained beyond dispute, proves by a mass of evidence in daily life how true were Lambert's deductions as to Action and Reaction.

The inner Being, the Being of Action—the word he used to designate an unknown specialization—the mysterious nexus of fibrils to which we owe the inadequately investigated powers of thought and will—in short, the nameless entity which sees, acts, foresees the end, and accomplishes everything before expressing itself in any physical phenomenon—must, in conformity with its nature, be free from the physical conditions by which the external Being of Reaction, the visible man, is fettered in its manifestation. From this followed a multitude of logical explanation as to those results of our twofold nature which appear the strangest, and a rectification of various systems in which truth and falsehood are mingled.

Certain men, having had a glimpse of some phenomena of the natural working of the Being of Action, were, like Swedenborg, carried away above this world by their ardent soul, thirsting for poetry, and filled with the Divine Spirit. Thus, in their ignorance of the causes and their admiration of the facts, they pleased their fancy by regarding that inner man as divine, and constructing a mystical universe. Hence we have angels! A lovely illusion which Lambert would never abandon, cherishing it even when the sword of his logic was cutting off their dazzling wings.

"Heaven," he would say, "must, after all, be the survival of our perfected faculties, and hell the void into which our unperfected faculties are cast away."

But how, then, in the ages when the understanding had preserved the religious and spiritualist impressions, which prevailed from the time of Christ till that of Descartes, between faith and doubt, how could men help accounting for the mysteries of our nature otherwise than by divine interposition? Of whom but of God Himself could sages demand an account of an invisible creature so actively and so reactively sensitive, gifted with faculties so extensive, so improvable by use, and so powerful under certain occult influences, that they could sometimes see it annihilate, by some phenomenon of sight or movement, space in its two manifestations—Time and Distance—of which the former is the space of the intellect, the latter is physical space? Sometimes they found it reconstructing the past, either by the power of retrospective vision, or by the mystery of a palingenesis not unlike the power a man might have of detecting in the form, integument, and embryo in a seed, the flowers of the past, and the numberless variations of their color, scent, and shape; and sometimes, again, it could be seen vaguely foreseeing the future, either by its apprehension of final causes, or by some phenomenon of physical presentiment.

Other men, less poetically religious, cold, and argumentative—quacks perhaps, but enthusiasts in brain at least, if not in heart — recognizing some isolated examples of such phenomena, admitted their truth while refusing to consider them as radiating from a common centre. Each of these was, then, bent on constructing a science out of a simple fact. Hence arose demonology, judicial astrology, the black arts, in short, every form of divination founded on circumstances that were essentially transient, because they varied according to men's temperament, and to conditions that are still completely unknown.

But from these errors of the learned, and from the ecclesiastical trials under which fell so many martyrs to their own powers, startling evidence was derived of the prodigious faculties at the command of the Being of Action, which, according to Lambert, can abstract itself completely from the Being of Reaction, bursting its envelope, and piercing walls by its potent vision; a phenomenon known to the Hindoos, as missionaries tell us, by the name of Tokeiad; or again, by another faculty, can grasp in the brain, in spite of its closest convolutions, the ideas which are formed or forming there, and the whole of past consciousness.

"If apparitions are not impossible," said Lambert, "they must be due to a faculty of discerning the ideas which represent man in his purest essence, whose life, imperishable perhaps, escapes our grosser senses, though they may become perceptible to the inner being when it has reached a high degree of ecstasy, or a great perfection of vision."

I know—though my remembrance is now vague—that Lambert, by following the results of Mind and Will step by step, after he had established their laws, accounted for a multitude of phenomena which, till then, had been regarded with reason as incomprehensible. Thus wizards, men possessed with second sight, and demoniacs of every degree—the victims of the Middle Ages— became the subject of explanations so natural, that their very simplicity often seemed to me the seal of their truth. The marvelous gifts which the Church of Rome, jealous of all mysteries, punished with the stake, were, in Louis' opinion, the result of certain affinities between the constituent elements of matter and those of mind, which proceed from the same source. The man holding a hazel rod when he found a spring of water was guided by some antipathy or sympathy of which he was unconscious; nothing but the eccentricity of these phenomena could have availed to give some of them historic certainty.

Sympathies have rarely been proved; they afford a kind of pleasure which those who are so happy as to possess them rarely speak of unless they are abnormally singular, and even then only in the privacy of intimate intercourse, where everything is buried. But the antipathies that arise from the inversion of affinities have, very happily, been recorded when developed by famous men. Thus, Bayle had hysterics when he heard water splashing, Scaliger turned pale at the sight of water-cress, Erasmus was thrown into a fever by the smell of fish. These three antipathies were connected with water. The Duc d'Epernon fainted at the sight of a hare, Tycho-Brahe at that of a fox, Henri III. at the presence of a cat, the Marechal d'Albret at the sight of a wild hog; these antipathies were produced by animal emanations, and often took effect at a great distance. The Chevalier de Guise, Marie de Medici, and many other persons have felt faint at seeing a rose even in a painting. Lord Bacon, whether he were forewarned or no of an eclipse of the moon, always fell into a syncope while it lasted; and his vitality, suspended while the phenomenon lasted was restored as soon as it was over without his feeling any further inconvenience. These effects of antipathy, all well authenticated, and chosen from among many which history has happened to preserve, are enough to give a clue to the sympathies which remain unknown.

This fragment of Lambert's investigations, which I remember from among his essays, will throw a light on the method on which he worked. I need not emphasize the obvious connection between this theory and the collateral sciences projected by Gall and Lavater; they were its natural corollary; and every more or less scientific brain will discern the ramifications by which it is inevitably connected with the phrenological observations of one and the speculations on physiognomy of the other.

Mesmer's discovery, so important, though as yet so little appreciated, was also embodied in a single section of this treatise, though Louis did not know the Swiss doctor's writings—which are few and brief.

A simple and logical inference from these principles led him to perceive that the will might be accumulated by a contractile effort of the inner man, and then, by another effort, projected, or even imparted, to material objects. Thus the whole force of a man must have the property of reacting on other men, and of infusing into them an essence foreign to their own, if they could not protect themselves against such an aggression. The evidence of this theorem of the science of humanity is, of course, very multifarious; but there is nothing to establish it beyond question. We have only the notorious disaster of Marius and his harangue to the Cimbrian commanded to kill him, or the august injunction of a mother to the Lion of Florence, in historic proof of instances of such lightning flashes of mind. To Lambert, then, Will and Thought were living forces; and he spoke of them in such a way as to impress his belief on the hearer. To him these two forces were, in a way, visible, tangible. Thought was slow or alert, heavy or nimble, light or dark; he ascribed to it all the attributes of an active agent, and thought of it as rising, resting, waking, expanding, growing old, shrinking, becoming atrophied, or resuscitating; he described its life, and specified all its actions by the strangest words in our language, speaking of its spontaneity, its strength, and all its qualities with a kind of intuition which enabled him to recognize all the manifestations of its substantial existence.

"Often," said he, "in the midst of quiet and silence, when our inner faculties are dormant, when a sort of darkness reigns within us, and we are lost in the contemplation of things outside us, an idea suddenly flies forth, and rushes with the swiftness of lightning across the infinite space which our inner vision allows us to perceive. This radiant idea, springing into existence like a will-o'-the-wisp, dies out never to return; an ephemeral life, like that of babes who give their parents such infinite joy and sorrow; a sort of still-born blossom in the fields of the mind. Sometimes an idea, instead of springing forcibly into life and dying unembodied, dawns gradually, hovers in the unknown limbo of the organs where it has its birth; exhausts us by long gestation, develops, is itself fruitful, grows outwardly in all the grace of youth and the promising attributes of a long life; it can endure the closest inspection, invites it, and never tires the sight; the investigation it undergoes commands the admiration we give to works slowly elaborated. Sometimes ideas are evolved in a swarm; one brings another; they come linked together; they vie with each other; they fly in clouds, wild and headlong. Again, they rise up pallid and misty, and perish for want of strength or of nutrition; the vital force is lacking. Or again, on certain days, they rush down into the depths to light up that immense obscurity; they terrify us and leave the soul dejected.

"Ideas are a complete system within us, resembling a natural kingdom, a sort of flora, of which the iconography will one day be outlined by some man who will perhaps be accounted a madman.

"Yes, within us and without, everything testifies to the livingness of those exquisite creations, which I compare with flowers in obedience to some unutterable revelation of their true nature!

"Their being produced as the final cause of man is, after all, not more amazing than the production of perfume and color in a plant. Perfumes are ideas, perhaps!

"When we consider the line where flesh ends and the nail begins contains the invisible and inexplicable mystery of the constant transformation of a fluid into horn, we must confess that nothing is impossible in the marvelous modifications of human tissue.

"And are there not in our inner nature phenomena of weight and motion comparable to those of physical nature? Suspense, to choose an example vividly familiar to everybody, is painful only as a result of the law in virtue of which the weight of a body is multiplied by its velocity. The weight of the feeling produced by suspense increases by the constant addition of past pain to the pain of the moment.

"And then, to what, unless it be to the electric fluid, are we to attribute the magic by which the Will enthrones itself so imperiously in the eye to demolish obstacles at the behest of genius, thunders in the voice, or filters, in spite of dissimulation, through the human frame? The current of that sovereign fluid, which, in obedience to the high pressure of thought or of feeling, flows in a torrent or is reduced to a mere thread, and collects to flash in lightnings, is the occult agent to which are due the evil or the beneficent efforts of Art and Passion—intonation of voice, whether harsh or suave, terrible, lascivious, horrifying or seductive by turns, thrilling the heart, the nerves, or the brain at our will; the marvels of the touch, the instrument of the mental transfusions of a myriad artists, whose creative fingers are able, after passionate study, to reproduce the forms of nature; or, again, the infinite gradations of the eye from dull inertia to the emission of the most terrifying gleams.

"By this system God is bereft of none of His rights. Mind, as a form of matter, has brought me a new conviction of His greatness."

After hearing him discourse thus, after receiving into my soul his look like a ray of light, it was difficult not to be dazzled by his conviction and carried away by his arguments. The Mind appeared to me as a purely physical power, surrounded by its innumerable progeny. It was a new conception of humanity under a new form.

This brief sketch of the laws which, as Lambert maintained, constitute the formula of our intellect, must suffice to give a notion of the prodigious activity of his spirit feeding on itself. Louis had sought for proofs of his theories in the history of great men, whose lives, as set forth by their biographers, supply very curious particulars as to the operation of their understanding. His memory allowed him to recall such facts as might serve to support his statements; he had appended them to each chapter in the form of demonstrations, so as to give to many of his theories an almost mathematical certainty. The works of Cardan, a man gifted with singular powers of insight, supplied him with valuable materials. He had not forgotten that Apollonius of Tyana had, in Asia, announced the death of a tyrant with every detail of his execution, at the very hour when it was taking place in Rome; nor that Plotinus, when far away from Porphyrius, was aware of his friend's intention to kill himself, and flew to dissuade him; nor the incident in the last century, proved in the face of the most incredulous mockery ever known—an incident most surprising to men who were accustomed to regard doubt as a weapon against the fact alone, but simple enough to believers—the fact that Alphonzo-Maria di Liguori, Bishop of Saint-Agatha, administered consolations to Pope Ganganelli, who saw him, heard him, and answered him, while the Bishop himself, at a great distance from Rome, was in a trance at home, in the chair where he commonly sat on his return from Mass. On recovering consciousness, he saw all his attendants kneeling beside him, believing him to be dead: "My friends," said he, "the Holy Father is just dead." Two days later a letter confirmed the news. The hour of the Pope's death coincided with that when the Bishop had been restored to his natural state.

Nor had Lambert omitted the yet more recent adventure of an English girl who was passionately attached to a sailor, and set out from London to seek him. She found him, without a guide, making her way alone in the North American wilderness, reaching him just in time to save his life.

Louis had found confirmatory evidence in the mysteries of the ancients, in the acts of the martyrs—in which glorious instances may be found of the triumph of human will, in the demonology of the Middle Ages, in criminal trials and medical researches; always selecting the real fact, the probable phenomenon, with admirable sagacity.

All this rich collection of scientific anecdotes, culled from so many books, most of them worthy of credit, served no doubt to wrap parcels in; and this work, which was curious, to say the least of it, as the outcome of a most extraordinary memory, was doomed to destruction.

Among the various cases which added to the value of Lambert's Treatise was an incident that had taken place in his own family, of which he had told me before he wrote his essay. This fact, bearing on the post-existence of the inner man, if I may be allowed to coin a new word for a phenomenon hitherto nameless, struck me so forcibly that I have never forgotten it. His father and mother were being forced into a lawsuit, of which the loss would leave them with a stain on their good name, the only thing they had in the world. Hence their anxiety was very great when the question first arose as to whether they should yield to the plaintiff's unjust demands, or should defend themselves against him. The matter came under discussion one autumn evening, before a turf fire in the room used by the tanner and his wife. Two or three relations were invited to this family council, and among others Louis' maternal great-grandfather, an old laborer, much bent, but with a venerable and dignified countenance, bright eyes, and a bald, yellow head, on which grew a few locks of thin, white hair. Like the Obi of the Negroes, or the Sagamore of the Indian savages, he was a sort of oracle, consulted on important occasions. His land was tilled by his grandchildren, who fed and served him; he predicted rain and fine weather, and told them when to mow the hay and gather the crops. The barometric exactitude of his forecasts was quite famous, and added to the confidence and respect he inspired. For whole days he would sit immovable in his armchair. This state of rapt meditation often came upon him since his wife's death; he had been attached to her in the truest and most faithful affection.

This discussion was held in his presence, but he did not seem to give much heed to it.

"My children," said he, when he was asked for his opinion, "this is too serious a matter for me to decide on alone. I must go and consult my wife."

The old man rose, took his stick, and went out, to the great astonishment of the others, who thought him daft. He presently came back and said:

"I did not have to go so far as the graveyard; your mother came to meet me; I found her by the brook. She tells me that you will find some receipts in the hands of a notary at Blois, which will enable you to gain your suit."

The words were spoken in a firm tone; the old man's demeanor and countenance showed that such an apparition was habitual with him. In fact, the disputed receipts were found, and the lawsuit was not attempted.

This event, under his father's roof and to his own knowledge, when Louis was nine years old, contributed largely to his belief in Swedenborg's miraculous visions, for in the course of that philosopher's life he repeatedly gave proof of the power of sight developed in his Inner Being. As he grew older, and as his intelligence was developed, Lambert was naturally led to seek in the laws of nature for the causes of the miracle which, in his childhood, had captivated his attention. What name can be given to the chance which brought within his ken so many facts and books bearing on such phenomena, and made him the principal subject and actor in such marvelous manifestations of mind?

If Lambert had no other title to fame than the fact of his having formulated, in his sixteenth year, such a psychological dictum as this:—"The events which bear witness to the action of the human race, and are the outcome of its intellect, have causes by which they are preconceived, as our actions are accomplished in our minds before they are reproduced by the outer man; presentiments or predictions are the perception of these causes"—I think we may deplore in him a genius equal to Pascal, Lavoisier, or Laplace. His chimerical notions about angels perhaps overruled his work too long; but was it not in trying to make gold that the alchemists unconsciously created chemistry? At the same time, Lambert, at a later period, studied comparative anatomy, physics, geometry, and other sciences bearing on his discoveries, and this was undoubtedly with the purpose of collecting facts and submitting them to analysis—the only torch that can guide us through the dark places of the most inscrutable work of nature. He had too much good sense to dwell among the clouds of theories which can all be expressed in a few words. In our day, is not the simplest demonstration based on facts more highly esteemed than the most specious system though defended by more or less ingenious inductions? But as I did not know him at the period of his life when his cogitations were, no doubt, the most productive of results, I can only conjecture that the bent of his work must have been from that of his first efforts of thought.

It is easy to see where his Treatise on the Will was faulty. Though gifted already with the powers which characterize superior men, he was but a boy. His brain, though endowed with a great faculty for abstractions, was still full of the delightful beliefs that hover around youth. Thus his conception, while at some points it touched the ripest fruits of his genius, still, by many more, clung to the smaller elements of its germs. To certain readers, lovers of poetry, what he chiefly lacked must have been a certain vein of interest.

But his work bore the stamp of the struggle that was going on in that noble Spirit between the two great principles of Spiritualism and Materialism, round which so many a fine genius has beaten its way without ever daring to amalgamate them. Louis, at first purely Spiritualist, had been irresistibly led to recognize the Material conditions of Mind. Confounded by the facts of analysis at the moment when his heart still gazed with yearning at the clouds which floated in Swedenborg's heaven, he had not yet acquired the necessary powers to produce a coherent system, compactly cast in a piece, as it were. Hence certain inconsistencies that have left their stamp even on the sketch here given of his first attempts. Still, incomplete as his work may have been, was it not the rough copy of a science of which he would have investigated the secrets at a later time, have secured the foundations, have examined, deduced, and connected the logical sequence?

Six months after the confiscation of the Treatise on the Will I left school. Our parting was unexpected. My mother, alarmed by a feverish attack which for some months I had been unable to shake off, while my inactive life induced symptoms of coma, carried me off at four or five hours' notice. The announcement of my departure reduced Lambert to dreadful dejection.

"Shall I ever seen you again?" said he in his gentle voice, as he clasped me in his arms. "You will live," he went on, "but I shall die. If I can, I will come back to you."

Only the young can utter such words with the accent of conviction that gives them the impressiveness of prophecy, of a pledge, leaving a terror of its fulfilment. For a long time indeed I vaguely looked for the promised apparition. Even now there are days of depression, of doubt, alarm, and loneliness, when I am forced to repel the intrusion of that sad parting, though it was not fated to be the last.

When I crossed the yard by which we left, Lambert was at one of the refectory windows to see me pass. By my request my mother obtained leave for him to dine with us at the inn, and in the evening I escorted him back to the fatal gate of the college. No lover and his mistress ever shed more tears at parting.

"Well, good-bye; I shall be left alone in this desert!" said he, pointing to the playground where two hundred boys were disporting themselves and shouting. "When I come back half dead with fatigue from my long excursions through the fields of thought, on whose heart can I rest? I could tell you everything in a look. Who will understand me now?—Good-bye! I could wish I had never met you; I should not know all I am losing."

"And what is to become of me?" said I. "Is not my position a dreadful one? I have nothing here to uphold me!" and I slapped my forehead.

He shook his head with a gentle gesture, gracious and sad, and we parted.

At that time Louis Lambert was about five feet five inches in height; he grew no more. His countenance, which was full of expression, revealed his sweet nature. Divine patience, developed by harsh usage, and the constant concentration needed for his meditative life, had bereft his eyes of the audacious pride which is so attractive in some faces, and which had so shocked our masters. Peaceful mildness gave charm to his face, an exquisite serenity that was never marred by a tinge of irony or satire; for his natural kindliness tempered his conscious strength and superiority. He had pretty hands, very slender, and almost always moist. His frame was a marvel, a model for a sculptor; but our iron-gray uniform, with gilt buttons and knee-breeches, gave us such an ungainly appearance that Lambert's fine proportions and firm muscles could only be appreciated in the bath. When we swam in our pool in the Loire, Louis was conspicuous by the whiteness of his skin, which was unlike the different shades of our schoolfellows' bodies mottled by the cold, or blue from the water. Gracefully formed, elegant in his attitudes, delicate in hue, never shivering after his bath, perhaps because he avoided the shade and always ran into the sunshine, Louis was like one of those cautious blossoms that close their petals to the blast and refuse to open unless to a clear sky. He ate little, and drank water only; either by instinct or by choice he was averse to any exertion that made a demand on his strength; his movements were few and simple, like those of Orientals or of savages, with whom gravity seems a condition of nature.

As a rule, he disliked everything that resembled any special care for his person. He commonly sat with his head a little inclined to the left, and so constantly rested his elbows on the table, that the sleeves of his coats were soon in holes.

To this slight picture of the outer man I must add a sketch of his moral qualities, for I believe I can now judge him impartially.

Though naturally religious, Louis did not accept the minute practices of the Roman ritual; his ideas were more intimately in sympathy with Saint Theresa and Fenelon, and several Fathers and certain Saints, who, in our day, would be regarded as heresiarchs or atheists. He was rigidly calm during the services. His own prayers went up in gusts, in aspirations, without any regular formality; in all things he gave himself up to nature, and would not pray, any more than he would think, at any fixed hour. In chapel he was equally apt to think of God or to meditate on some problem of philosophy.

To him Jesus Christ was the most perfect type of his system. Et Verbum caro factum est seemed a sublime statement intended to express the traditional formula of the Will, the Word, and the Act made visible. Christ's unconsciousness of His Death—having so perfected His inner Being by divine works, that one day the invisible form of it appeared to His disciples—and the other Mysteries of the Gospels, the magnetic cures wrought by Christ, and the gift of tongues, all to him confirmed his doctrine. I remember once hearing him say on this subject, that the greatest work that could be written nowadays was a History of the

Primitive Church. And he never rose to such poetic heights as when, in the evening, as we conversed, he would enter on an inquiry into miracles, worked by the power of Will during that great age of faith. He discerned the strongest evidence of his theory in most of the martyrdoms endured during the first century of our era, which he spoke of as the great era of the Mind.

"Do not the phenomena observed in almost every instance of the torments so heroically endured by the early Christians for the establishment of the faith, amply prove that Material force will never prevail against the force of Ideas or the Will of man?" he would say. "From this effect, produced by the Will of all, each man may draw conclusions in favor of his own."

I need say nothing of his views on poetry or history, nor of his judgment on the masterpieces of our language. There would be little interest in the record of opinions now almost universally held, though at that time, from the lips of a boy, they might seem remarkable. Louis was capable of the highest flights. To give a notion of his talents in a few words, he could have written Zadig as wittily as Voltaire; he could have thought out the dialogue between Sylla and Eucrates as powerfully as Montesquieu. His rectitude of character made him desire above all else in a work that it should bear the stamp of utility; at the same time, his refined taste demanded novelty of thought as well as of form. One of his most remarkable literary observations, which will serve as a clue to all the others, and show the lucidity of his judgment, is this, which has ever dwelt in my memory, "The Apocalypse is written ecstasy." He regarded the Bible as a part of the traditional history of the antediluvian nations which had taken for its share the new humanity. He thought that the mythology of the Greeks was borrowed both from the Hebrew Scriptures and from the sacred Books of India, adapted after their own fashion by the beauty-loving Hellenes.

"It is impossible," said he, "to doubt the priority of the Asiatic Scriptures; they are earlier than our sacred books. The man who is candid enough to admit this historical fact sees the whole world expand before him. Was it not on the Asiatic highland that the few men took refuge who were able to escape the catastrophe that ruined our globe—if, indeed men had existed before that cataclysm or shock? A serious query, the answer to which lies at the bottom of the sea. The anthropogony of the Bible is merely a genealogy of a swarm escaping from the human hive which settled on the mountainous slopes of Thibet between the summits of the Himalaya and the Caucasus.

"The character of the primitive ideas of that horde called by its lawgiver the people of God, no doubt to secure its unity, and perhaps also to induce it to maintain his laws and his system of government —for the Books of Moses are a religious, political, and civil code —that character bears the authority of terror; convulsions of nature are interpreted with stupendous power as a vengeance from on high. In fact, since this wandering tribe knew none of the ease enjoyed by a community settled in a patriarchal home, their sorrows as pilgrims inspired them with none but gloomy poems, majestic but blood-stained. In the Hindoos, on the contrary, the spectacle of the rapid recoveries of the natural world, and the prodigious effects of sunshine, which they were the first to recognize, gave rise to happy images of blissful love, to the worship of Fire and of the endless personifications of reproductive force. These fine fancies are lacking in the Book of the Hebrews. A constant need of self-preservation amid all the dangers and the lands they traversed to reach the Promised Land engendered their exclusive race-feeling and their hatred of all other nations.

"These three Scriptures are the archives of an engulfed world. Therein lies the secret of the extraordinary splendor of those languages and their myths. A grand human history lies beneath those names of men and places, and those fables which charm us so irresistibly, we know not why. Perhaps it is because we find in them the native air of renewed humanity."

Thus, to him, this threefold literature included all the thoughts of man. Not a book could be written, in his opinion, of which the subject might not there be discerned in its germ. This view shows how learnedly he had pursued his early studies of the Bible, and how far they had led him. Hovering, as it were, over the heads of society, and knowing it solely from books, he could judge it coldly.

"The law," said he, "never puts a check on the enterprises of the rich and great, but crushes the poor, who, on the contrary, need protection."

His kind heart did not therefore allow him to sympathize in political ideas; his system led rather to the passive obedience of which Jesus set the example. During the last hours of my life at Vendome, Louis had ceased to feel the spur to glory; he had, in a way, had an abstract enjoyment of fame; and having opened it, as the ancient priests of sacrifice sought to read the future in the hearts of men, he had found nothing in the entrails of his chimera. Scorning a sentiment so wholly personal: "Glory," said he, "is but beatified egoism."

Here, perhaps, before taking leave of this exceptional boyhood, I may pronounce judgment on it by a rapid glance.

A short time before our separation, Lambert said to me:

"Apart from the general laws which I have formulated—and this, perhaps, will be my glory—laws which must be those of the human organism, the life of man is Movement determined in each individual by the pressure of some inscrutable influence—by the brain, the heart, or the sinews. All the innumerable modes of human existence result from the proportions in which these three generating forces are more or less intimately combined with the substances they assimilate in the environment they live in."

He stopped short, struck his forehead, and exclaimed: "How strange! In every great man whose portrait I have remarked, the neck is short. Perhaps nature requires that in them the heart should be nearer to the brain!"

Then he went on:

"From that, a sum-total of action takes its rise which constitutes social life. The man of sinew contributes action or strength; the man of brain, genius; the man of heart, faith. But," he added sadly, "faith sees only the clouds of the sanctuary; the Angel alone has light."

So, according to his own definitions, Lambert was all brain and all heart. It seems to me that his intellectual life was divided into three marked phases.

Under the impulsion, from his earliest years, of a precocious activity, due, no doubt, to some malady—or to some special perfection—of organism, his powers were concentrated on the functions of the inner senses and a superabundant flow of nerve-fluid. As a man of ideas, he craved to satisfy the thirst of his brain, to assimilate every idea. Hence his reading; and from his reading, the reflections that gave him the power of reducing things to their simplest expression, and of absorbing them to study them in their essence. Thus, the advantages of this splendid stage, acquired by other men only after long study, were achieved by Lambert during his bodily childhood: a happy childhood, colored by the studious joys of a born poet.

The point which most thinkers reach at last was to him the starting-point, whence his brain was to set out one day in search of new worlds of knowledge. Though as yet he knew it not, he had made for himself the most exacting life possible, and the most insatiably greedy. Merely to live, was he not compelled to be perpetually casting nutriment into the gulf he had opened in himself? Like some beings who dwell in the grosser world, might not he die of inanition for want of feeding abnormal and disappointed cravings? Was not this a sort of debauchery of the intellect which might lead to spontaneous combustion, like that of bodies saturated with alcohol?

I had seen nothing of this first phase of his brain-development; it is only now, at a later day, that I can thus give an account of its prodigious fruit and results. Lambert was now thirteen.

I was so fortunate as to witness the first stage of the second period. Lambert was cast into all the miseries of school-life—and that, perhaps, was his salvation—it absorbed the superabundance of his thoughts. After passing from concrete ideas to their purest expression, from words to their ideal import, and from that import to principles, after reducing everything to the abstract, to enable him to live he yearned for yet other intellectual creations. Quelled by the woes of school and the critical development of his physical constitution, he became thoughtful, dreamed of feeling, and caught a glimpse of new sciences—positively masses of ideas. Checked in his career, and not yet strong enough to contemplate the higher spheres, he contemplated his inmost self. I then perceived in him the struggle of the Mind reacting on itself, and trying to detect the secrets of its own nature, like a physician who watches the course of his own disease.

At this stage of weakness and strength, of childish grace and superhuman powers, Louis Lambert is the creature who, more than any other, gave me a poetical and truthful image of the being we call an angel, always excepting one woman whose name, whose features, whose identity, and whose life I would fain hide from all the world, so as to be sole master of the secret of her existence, and to bury it in the depths of my heart.

The third phase I was not destined to see. It began when Lambert and I were parted, for he did not leave college till he was eighteen, in the summer of 1815. He had at that time lost his father and mother about six months before. Finding no member of his family with whom his soul could sympathize, expansive still, but, since our parting, thrown back on himself, he made his home with his uncle, who was also his guardian, and who, having been turned out of his benefice as a priest who had taken the oaths, had come to settle at Blois. There Louis lived for some time; but consumed ere long by the desire to finish his incomplete studies, he came to Paris to see Madame de Stael, and to drink of science at its highest fount. The old priest, being very fond of his nephew, left Louis free to spend his whole little inheritance in his three years' stay in Paris, though he lived very poorly. This fortune consisted of but a few thousand francs.

Lambert returned to Blois at the beginning of 1820, driven from Paris by the sufferings to which the impecunious are exposed there. He must often have been a victim to the secret storms, the terrible rage of mind by which artists are tossed to judge from the only fact his uncle recollected, and the only letter he preserved of all those which Louis Lambert wrote to him at that time, perhaps because it was the last and the longest.

To begin with the story. Louis one evening was at the Theatre-Francais, seated on a bench in the upper gallery, near to one of the pillars which, in those days, divided off the third row of boxes. On rising between the acts, he saw a young woman who had just come into the box next him. The sight of this lady, who was young, pretty, well dressed, in a low bodice no doubt, and escorted by a man for whom her face beamed with all the charms of love, produced such a terrible effect on Lambert's soul and senses, that he was obliged to leave the theatre. If he had not been controlled by some remaining glimmer of reason, which was not wholly extinguished by this first fever of burning passion, he might perhaps have yielded to the most irresistible desire that came over him to kill the young man on whom the lady's looks beamed. Was not this a reversion, in the heart of the Paris world, to the savage passion that regards women as its prey, an effect of animal instinct combining with the almost luminous flashes of a soul crushed under the weight of thought? In short, was it not the prick of the penknife so vividly imagined by the boy, felt by the man as the thunderbolt of his most vital craving—for love?

And now, here is the letter that depicts the state of his mind as it was struck by the spectacle of Parisian civilization. His feelings, perpetually wounded no doubt in that whirlpool of self-interest, must always have suffered there; he probably had no friend to comfort him, no enemy to give tone to this life. Compelled to live in himself alone, having no one to share his subtle raptures, he may have hoped to solve the problem of his destiny by a life of ecstasy, adopting an almost vegetative attitude, like an anchorite of the early Church, and abdicating the empire of the intellectual world.

This letter seems to hint at such a scheme, which is a temptation to all lofty souls at periods of social reform. But is not this purpose, in some cases, the result of a vocation? Do not some of them endeavor to concentrate their powers by long silence, so as to emerge fully capable of governing the world by word or by deed? Louis must, assuredly, have found much bitterness in his intercourse with men, or have striven hard with Society in terrible irony, without extracting anything from it, before uttering so strident a cry, and expressing, poor fellow, the desire which satiety of power and of all earthly things has led even monarchs to indulge!

And perhaps, too, he went back to solitude to carry out some great work that was floating inchoate in his brain. We would gladly believe it as we read this fragment of his thoughts, betraying the struggle of his soul at the time when youth was ending and the terrible power of production was coming into being, to which we might have owed the works of the man.

This letter connects itself with the adventure at the theatre. The incident and the letter throw light on each other, body and soul were tuned to the same pitch. This tempest of doubts and asseverations, of clouds and of lightnings that flash before the thunder, ending by a starved yearning for heavenly illumination, throws such a light on the third phase of his education as enables us to understand it perfectly. As we read these lines, written at chance moments, taken up when the vicissitudes of life in Paris allowed, may we not fancy that we see an oak at that stage of its growth when its inner expansion bursts the tender green bark, covering it with wrinkles and cracks, when its majestic stature is in preparation—if indeed the lightnings of heaven and the axe of man shall spare it?

This letter, then, will close, alike for the poet and the philosopher, this portentous childhood and unappreciated youth. It finishes off the outline of this nature in its germ. Philosophers will regret the foliage frost-nipped in the bud; but they will, perhaps, find the flowers expanding in regions far above the highest places of the earth.

"PARIS, September-October 1819.

"DEAR UNCLE, – I shall soon be leaving this part of the world, where I could never bear to live. I find no one here who likes what I like, who works at my work, or is amazed at what amazes me. Thrown back on myself, I eat my heart out in misery. My long and patient study of Society here has brought me to melancholy conclusions, in which doubt predominates.

"Here, money is the mainspring of everything. Money is indispensable, even for going without money. But though that dross is necessary to any one who wishes to think in peace, I have not courage enough to make it the sole motive power of my thoughts. To make a fortune, I must take up a profession; in two words, I must, by acquiring some privilege of position or of self-advertisement, either legal or ingeniously contrived, purchase the right of taking day by day out of somebody else's purse a certain sum which, by the end of the year, would

amount to a small capital; and this, in twenty years, would hardly secure an income of four or five thousand francs to a man who deals honestly. An advocate, a notary, a merchant, any recognized professional, has earned a living for his later days in the course of fifteen or sixteen years after ending his apprenticeship.

"But I have never felt fit for work of this kind. I prefer thought to action, an idea to a transaction, contemplation to activity. I am absolutely devoid of the constant attention indispensable to the making of a fortune. Any mercantile venture, any need for using other people's money would bring me to grief, and I should be ruined. Though I have nothing, at least at the moment, I owe nothing. The man who gives his life to the achievement of great things in the sphere of intellect, needs very little; still, though twenty sous a day would be enough, I do not possess that small income for my laborious idleness. When I wish to cogitate, want drives me out of the sanctuary where my mind has its being. What is to become of me?

"I am not frightened at poverty. If it were not that beggars are imprisoned, branded, scorned, I would beg, to enable me to solve at my leisure the problems that haunt me. Still, this sublime resignation, by which I might emancipate my mind, through abstracting it from the body, would not serve my end. I should still need money to devote myself to certain experiments. But for that, I would accept the outward indigence of a sage possessed of both heaven and heart. A man need only never stoop, to remain lofty in poverty. He who struggles and endures, while marching on to a glorious end, presents a noble spectacle; but who can have the strength to fight here? We can climb cliffs, but it is unendurable to remain for ever tramping the mud. Everything here checks the flight of the spirit that strives towards the future.

"I should not be afraid of myself in a desert cave; I am afraid of myself here. In the desert I should be alone with myself, undisturbed; here man has a thousand wants which drag him down. You go out walking, absorbed in dreams; the voice of the beggar asking an alms brings you back to this world of hunger and thirst. You need money only to take a walk. Your organs of sense, perpetually wearied by trifles, never get any rest. The poet's sensitive nerves are perpetually shocked, and what ought to be his glory becomes his torment; his imagination is his cruelest enemy. The injured workman, the poor mother in childbed, the prostitute who has

fallen ill, the foundling, the infirm and aged—even vice and crime here find a refuge and charity; but the world is merciless to the inventor, to the man who thinks. Here everything must show an immediate and practical result. Fruitless attempts are mocked at, though they may lead to the greatest discoveries; the deep and untiring study that demands long concentrations of every faculty is not valued here. The State might pay talent as it pays the bayonet; but it is afraid of being taken in by mere cleverness, as if genius could be counterfeited for any length of time.

"Ah, my dear uncle, when monastic solitude was destroyed, uprooted from its home at the foot of mountains, under green and silent shade, asylums ought to have been provided for those suffering souls who, by an idea, promote the progress of nations or prepare some new and fruitful development of science.

"September 20th.

"The love of study brought me hither, as you know. I have met really learned men, amazing for the most part; but the lack of unity in scientific work almost nullifies their efforts. There is no Head of instruction or of scientific research. At the Museum a professor argues to prove that another in the Rue Saint-Jacques talks nonsense. The lecturer at the College of Medicine abuses him of the College de France. When I first arrived, I went to hear an old Academician who taught five hundred youths that Corneille was a haughty and powerful genius; Racine, elegiac and graceful; Moliere, inimitable; Voltaire, supremely witty; Bossuet and Pascal, incomparable in argument. A professor of philosophy may make a name by explaining how Plato is Platonic. Another discourses on the history of words, without troubling himself about ideas. One explains Aeschylus, another tells you that communes were communes, and neither more nor less. These original and brilliant discoveries, diluted to last several hours, constitute the higher education which is to lead to giant strides in human knowledge.

"If the Government could have an idea, I should suspect it of being afraid of any real superiority, which, once roused, might bring Society under the yoke of an intelligent rule. Then nations would go too far and too fast; so professors are appointed to produce simpletons. How else can we account for a scheme devoid of method or any notion of the future?

"The Institut might be the central government of the moral and intellectual world; but it has been ruined lately by its subdivision into separate academies. So human science marches on, without a guide, without a system, and floats haphazard with no road traced out.

"This vagueness and uncertainty prevails in politics as well as in science. In the order of nature means are simple, the end is grand and marvelous; here in science as in government, the means are stupendous, the end is mean. The force which in nature proceeds at an equal pace, and of which the sum is constantly being added to itself—the A + A from which everything is produced—is destructive in society. Politics, at the present time, place human forces in antagonism to neutralize each other, instead of combining them to promote their action to some definite end.

"Looking at Europe alone, from Caesar to Constantine, from the puny Constantine to the great Attila, from the Huns to Charlemagne, from Charlemagne to Leo X., from Leo X., to Philip II., from Philip II. to Louis XIV.; from Venice to England, from England to Napoleon, from Napoleon to England, I see no fixed purpose in politics; its constant agitation has led to no progress.

"Nations leave witnesses to their greatness in monuments, and to their happiness in the welfare of individuals. Are modern monuments as fine as those of the ancients? I doubt it. The arts, which are the direct outcome of the individual, the products of genius or of handicraft, have not advanced much. The pleasures of Lucullus were as good as those of Samuel Bernard, of Beaujon, or of the King of Bavaria. And then human longevity has diminished.

"Thus, to those who will be candid, man is still the same; might is his only law, and success his only wisdom.

"Jesus Christ, Mahomet, and Luther only lent a different hue to the arena in which youthful nations disport themselves.

"No development of politics has hindered civilization, with its riches, its manners, its alliance of the strong against the weak, its ideas, and its delights, from moving from Memphis to Tyre, from Tyre to Baalbek, from Tadmor to Carthage, from Carthage to Rome, from Rome to Constantinople, from Constantinople to Venice, from Venice to Spain, from Spain to England—while no trace is left of Memphis, of Tyre, of Carthage, of Rome, of Venice, or Madrid. The soul of those great bodies has fled. Not one of them has preserved itself from destruction, nor formulated

this axiom: When the effect produced ceases to be in a ratio to its cause, disorganization follows.

"The most subtle genius can discover no common bond between great social facts. No political theory has ever lasted. Governments pass away, as men do, without handing down any lesson, and no system gives birth to a system better than that which came before it. What can we say about politics when a Government directly referred to God perished in India and Egypt; when the rule of the Sword and of the Tiara are past; when Monarchy is dying; when the Government of the People has never been alive; when no scheme of intellectual power as applied to material interests has ever proved durable, and everything at this day remains to be done all over again, as it has been at every period when man has turned to cry out, 'I am in torment!'

"The code, which is considered Napoleon's greatest achievement, is the most Draconian work I know of. Territorial subdivision carried out to the uttermost, and its principle confirmed by the equal division of property generally, must result in the degeneracy of the nation and the death of the Arts and Sciences. The land, too much broken up, is cultivated only with cereals and small crops; the forests, and consequently the rivers, are disappearing; oxen and horses are no longer bred. Means are lacking both for attack and for resistance. If we should be invaded, the people must be crushed; it has lost its mainspring—its leaders. This is the history of deserts!

"Thus the science of politics has no definite principles, and it can have no fixity; it is the spirit of the hour, the perpetual application of strength proportioned to the necessities of the moment. The man who should foresee two centuries ahead would die on the place of execution, loaded with the imprecations of the mob, or else—which seems worse—would be lashed with the myriad whips of ridicule. Nations are but individuals, neither wiser nor stronger than man, and their destinies are identical. If we reflect on man, is not that to consider mankind?

"By studying the spectacle of society perpetually storm-tossed in its foundations as well as in its results, in its causes as well as in its actions, while philanthropy is but a splendid mistake, and progress is vanity, I have been confirmed in this truth: Life is within and not without us; to rise above men, to govern them, is only the part of an aggrandized school-

master; and those men who are capable of rising to the level whence they can enjoy a view of the world should not look at their own feet.

"November 4th.

"I am no doubt occupied with weighty thoughts, I am on the way to certain discoveries, an invincible power bears me toward a luminary which shone at an early age on the darkness of my moral life; but what name can I give to the power that ties my hands and shuts my mouth, and drags me in a direction opposite to my vocation? I must leave Paris, bid farewell to the books in the libraries, those noble centres of illumination, those kindly and always accessible sages, and the younger geniuses with whom I sympathize. Who is it that drives me away? Chance or Providence?

"The two ideas represented by those words are irreconcilable. If Chance does not exist, we must admit fatalism, that is to say, the compulsory co-ordination of things under the rule of a general plan. Why then do we rebel? If man is not free, what becomes of the scaffolding of his moral sense? Or, if he can control his destiny, if by his own freewill he can interfere with the execution of the general plan, what becomes of God?

"Why did I come here? If I examine myself, I find the answer: I find in myself axioms that need developing. But why then have I such vast faculties without being suffered to use them? If my suffering could serve as an example, I could understand it; but no, I suffer unknown.

"This is perhaps as much the act of Providence as the fate of the flower that dies unseen in the heart of the virgin forest, where no one can enjoy its perfume or admire its splendor. Just as that blossom vainly sheds its fragrance to the solitude, so do I, here in the garret, give birth to ideas that no one can grasp.

"Yesterday evening I sat eating bread and grapes in front of my window with a young doctor named Meyraux. We talked as men do whom misfortune has joined in brotherhood, and I said to him:

"'I am going away; you are staying. Take up my ideas and develop them.'

"'I cannot!' said he, with bitter regret: 'my feeble health cannot stand so much work, and I shall die young of my struggle with penury.'

"We looked up at the sky and grasped hands. We first met at the

Comparative Anatomy course, and in the galleries of the Museum, attracted thither by the same study—the unity of geological structure. In him this was the presentiment of genius sent to open a new path in the fallows of intellect; in me it was a deduction from a general system.

"My point is to ascertain the real relation that may exist between God and man. Is not this a need of the age? Without the highest assurance, it is impossible to put bit and bridle on the social factions that have been let loose by the spirit of scepticism and discussion, and which are now crying aloud: 'Show us a way in which we may walk and find no pitfalls in our way!'

"You will wonder what comparative anatomy has to do with a question of such importance to the future of society. Must we not attain to the conviction that man is the end of all earthly means before we ask whether he too is not the means to some end? If man is bound up with everything, is there not something above him with which he again is bound up? If he is the end-all of the explained transmutations that lead up to him, must he not be also the link between the visible and invisible creations?

"The activity of the universe is not absurd; it must tend to an end, and that end is surely not a social body constituted as ours is! There is a fearful gulf between us and heaven. In our present existence we can neither be always happy nor always in torment; must there not be some tremendous change to bring about Paradise and Hell, two images without which God cannot exist to the mind of the vulgar? I know that a compromise was made by the invention of the Soul; but it is repugnant to me to make God answerable for human baseness, for our disenchantments, our aversions, our degeneracy.

"Again, how can we recognize as divine the principle within us which can be overthrown by a few glasses of rum? How conceive of immaterial faculties which matter can conquer, and whose exercise is suspended by a grain of opium? How imagine that we shall be able to feel when we are bereft of the vehicles of sensation? Why must God perish if matter can be proved to think? Is the vitality of matter in its innumerable manifestations—the effect of its instincts—at all more explicable than the effects of the mind? Is not the motion given to the worlds enough to prove God's existence, without our plunging into absurd speculations suggested by pride? And if we pass, after our trials, from a perishable state of being to a higher existence, is not that enough for a creature that is distinguished

from other creatures only by more perfect instincts? If in moral philosophy there is not a single principle which does not lead to the absurd, or cannot be disproved by evidence, is it not high time that we should set to work to seek such dogmas as are written in the innermost nature of things? Must we not reverse philosophical science?

"We trouble ourselves very little about the supposed void that must have pre-existed for us, and we try to fathom the supposed void that lies before us. We make God responsible for the future, but we do not expect Him to account for the past. And yet it is quite as desirable to know whether we have any roots in the past as to discover whether we are inseparable from the future.

"We have been Deists or Atheists in one direction only.

"Is the world eternal? Was the world created? We can conceive of no middle term between these two propositions; one, then, is true and the other false! Take your choice. Whichever it may be, God, as our reason depicts Him, must be deposed, and that amounts to denial. The world is eternal: then, beyond question, God has had it forced upon Him. The world was created: then God is an impossibility. How could He have subsisted through an eternity, not knowing that He would presently want to create the world? How could He have failed to foresee all the results?

"Whence did He derive the essence of creation? Evidently from Himself. If, then, the world proceeds from God, how can you account for evil? That Evil should proceed from Good is absurd. If evil does not exist, what do you make of social life and its laws? On all hands we find a precipice! On every side a gulf in which reason is lost! Then social science must be altogether reconstructed.

"Listen to me, uncle; until some splendid genius shall have taken account of the obvious inequality of intellects and the general sense of humanity, the word God will be constantly arraigned, and Society will rest on shifting sands. The secret of the various moral zones through which man passes will be discovered by the analysis of the animal type as a whole. That animal type has hitherto been studied with reference only to its differences, not to its similitudes; in its organic manifestations, not in its faculties. Animal faculties are perfected in direct transmission, in obedience to laws which remain to be discovered. These faculties correspond to the forces which express them, and those forces are essentially material and divisible.

"Material faculties! Reflect on this juxtaposition of words. Is not this a problem as insoluble as that of the first communication of motion to matter—an unsounded gulf of which the difficulties were transposed rather than removed by Newton's system? Again, the universal assimilation of light by everything that exists on earth demands a new study of our globe. The same animal differs in the tropics of India and in the North. Under the angular or the vertical incidence of the sun's rays nature is developed the same, but not the same; identical in its principles, but totally dissimilar in its outcome. The phenomenon that amazes our eyes in the zoological world when we compare the butterflies of Brazil with those of Europe, is even more startling in the world of Mind. A particular facial angle, a certain amount of brain convolutions, are indispensable to produce Columbus, Raphael, Napoleon, Laplace, or Beethoven; the sunless valley produces the cretin—draw your own conclusions. Why such differences, due to the more or less ample diffusion of light to men? The masses of suffering humanity, more or less active, fed, and enlightened, are a difficulty to be accounted for, crying out against God.

"Why in great joy do we always want to quit the earth? Whence comes the longing to rise which every creature has known or will know? Motion is a great soul, and its alliance with matter is just as difficult to account for as the origin of thought in man. In these days science is one; it is impossible to touch politics independent of moral questions, and these are bound up with scientific questions. It seems to me that we are on the eve of a great human struggle; the forces are there; only I do not see the General.

"November 25.

"Believe me, dear uncle, it is hard to give up the life that is in us without a pang. I am returning to Blois with a heavy grip at my heart; I shall die then, taking with me some useful truths. No personal interest debases my regrets. Is earthly fame a guerdon to those who believe that they will mount to a higher sphere?

"I am by no means in love with the two syllables Lam and bert; whether spoken with respect or with contempt over my grave, they can make no change in my ultimate destiny. I feel myself strong and energetic; I might become a power; I feel in myself a life so luminous that it might

enlighten a world, and yet I am shut up in a sort of mineral, as perhaps indeed are the colors you admire on the neck of an Indian bird. I should need to embrace the whole world, to clasp and re-create it; but those who have done this,

who have thus embraced and remoulded it began—did they not?—by being a wheel in the machine. I can only be crushed. Mahomet had the sword; Jesus had the cross; I shall die unknown. I shall be at Blois for a day, and then in my coffin.

"Do you know why I have come back to Swedenborg after vast studies of all religions, and after proving to myself, by reading all the works published within the last sixty years by the patient English, by Germany, and by France, how deeply true were my youthful views about the Bible? Swedenborg undoubtedly epitomizes all the religions—or rather the one religion—of humanity. Though forms of worship are infinitely various, neither their true meaning nor their metaphysical interpretation has ever varied. In short, man has, and has had, but one religion.

"Sivaism, Vishnuism, and Brahmanism, the three primitive creeds, originating as they did in Thibet, in the valley of the Indus, and on the vast plains of the Ganges, ended their warfare some thousand years before the birth of Christ by adopting the Hindoo Trimourti. The Trimourti is our Trinity. From this dogma Magianism arose in Persia; in Egypt, the African beliefs and the Mosaic law; the worship of the Cabiri, and the polytheism of Greece and Rome. While by this ramification of the Trimourti the Asiatic myths became adapted to the imaginations of various races in the lands they reached by the agency of certain sages whom men elevated to be demi-gods—Mithra, Bacchus, Hermes, Hercules, and the rest —Buddha, the great reformer of the three primeval religions, lived in India, and founded his Church there, a sect which still numbers two hundred millions more believers than Christianity can show, while it certainly influenced the powerful Will both of Jesus and of Confucius.

"Then Christianity raised her standard. Subsequently Mahomet fused Judaism and Christianity, the Bible and the Gospel, in one book, the Koran, adapting them to the apprehension of the Arab race. Finally, Swedenborg borrowed from Magianism, Brahmanism, Buddhism, and Christian mysticism all the truth and divine beauty that those four great religious books hold in common, and added to them a doctrine, a basis of reasoning, that may be termed mathematical.

"Any man who plunges into these religious waters, of which the sources are not all known, will find proofs that Zoroaster, Moses, Buddha, Confucius, Jesus Christ, and Swedenborg had identical principles and aimed at identical ends.

"The last of them all, Swedenborg, will perhaps be the Buddha of the North. Obscure and diffuse as his writings are, we find in them the elements of a magnificent conception of society. His Theocracy is sublime, and his creed is the only acceptable one to superior souls. He alone brings man into immediate communion with God, he gives a thirst for God, he has freed the majesty of God from the trappings in which other human dogmas have disguised Him. He left Him where He is, making His myriad creations and creatures gravitate towards Him through successive transformations which promise a more immediate and more natural future than the Catholic idea of Eternity. Swedenborg has absolved God from the reproach attaching to Him in the estimation of tender souls for the perpetuity of revenge to punish the sin of a moment—a system of injustice and cruelty.

"Each man may know for himself what hope he has of life eternal, and whether this world has any rational sense. I mean to make the attempt. And this attempt may save the world, just as much as the cross at Jerusalem or the sword at Mecca. These were both the off spring of the desert. Of the thirty-three years of Christ's life, we only know the history of nine; His life of seclusion prepared Him for His life of glory. And I too crave for the desert!"

Notwithstanding the difficulties of the task, I have felt it my duty to depict Lambert's boyhood, the unknown life to which I owe the only happy hours, the only pleasant memories, of my early days. Excepting during those two years I had nothing but annoyances and weariness. Though some happiness was mine at a later time, it was always incomplete.

I have been diffuse, I know; but in default of entering into the whole wide heart and brain of Louis Lambert—two words which inadequately express the infinite aspects of his inner life—it would be almost impossible to make the second part of his intellectual history intelligible—a phase that was unknown to the world and to me, but of which the mystical outcome was made evident to my eyes in the course of a few hours. Those who have not already dropped this volume, will, I hope, understand the events I still have to tell, forming as they do a sort of second existence lived by this creature—may I not say this creation?—in whom everything was to be so extraordinary, even his end.

When Louis returned to Blois, his uncle was eager to procure him some amusement; but the poor priest was regarded as a perfect leper in that godly-minded town. No one would have anything to say to a revolutionary who had taken the oaths. His society, therefore, consisted of a few individuals of what were then called liberal or patriotic, or constitutional opinions, on whom he would call for a rubber of whist or of boston.

At the first house where he was introduced by his uncle, Louis met a young lady, whose circumstances obliged her to remain in this circle, so contemned by those of the fashionable world, though her fortune was such as to make it probable that she might by and by marry into the highest aristocracy of the province. Mademoiselle Pauline de Villenoix was sole heiress to the wealth amassed by her grandfather, a Jew named Salomon, who, contrary to the customs of his nation, had, in his old age, married a Christian and a Catholic. He had only one son, who was brought up in his mother's faith. At his father's death young Salomon purchased what was known at that time as a savonnette a vilain (literally a cake of soap for a serf), a small estate called Villenoix, which he contrived to get registered with a baronial title, and took its name. He died unmarried, but he left a natural daughter, to whom he bequeathed the greater part of his fortune, including the lands of Villenoix. He appointed one of his uncles, Monsieur Joseph Salomon, to be the girl's guardian. The old Jew was so devoted to his ward that he seemed willing to make great sacrifices for the sake of marrying her well. But Mademoiselle de Villenoix's birth, and the cherished prejudice against Jews that prevails in the provinces, would not allow of her being received in the very exclusive circle which, rightly or wrongly, considers itself noble, notwithstanding her own large fortune and her guardian's.

Monsieur Joseph Salomon was resolved that if she could not secure a country squire, his niece should go to Paris and make choice of a husband among the peers of France, liberal or monarchical; as to happiness, that he believed he could secure her by the terms of the marriage contract.

Mademoiselle de Villenoix was now twenty. Her remarkable beauty and gifts of mind were surer guarantees of happiness than those offered by money. Her features were of the purest type of Jewish beauty; the oval lines, so noble and maidenly, have an indescribable stamp of the ideal, and seem to speak of the joys of the East, its unchangeably blue sky, the glories of its lands, and the fabulous riches of life there. She had fine eyes, shaded by deep eyelids, fringed with thick, curled lashes. Biblical innocence sat on her brow. Her complexion was of the pure whiteness of the Levite's robe. She was habitually silent and thoughtful, but her movements and gestures betrayed a quiet grace, as her speech bore witness to a woman's sweet and loving nature. She had not, indeed, the rosy freshness, the fruit-like bloom which blush on a girl's cheek during her careless years. Darker shadows, with here and there a redder vein, took the place of color, symptomatic of an energetic temper and nervous irritability, such as many men do not like to meet with in a wife, while to others they are an indication of the most sensitive chastity and passion mingled with pride.

As soon as Louis saw Mademoiselle de Villenoix, he discerned the angel within. The richest powers of his soul, and his tendency to ecstatic reverie, every faculty within him was at once concentrated in boundless love, the first love of a young man, a passion which is strong indeed in all, but which in him was raised to incalculable power by the perennial ardor of his senses, the character of his ideas, and the manner in which he lived. This passion became a gulf, into which the hapless fellow threw everything; a gulf whither the mind dare not venture, since his, flexible and firm as it was, was lost there. There all was mysterious, for everything went on in that moral world, closed to most men, whose laws were revealed to him—perhaps to his sorrow.

When an accident threw me in the way of his uncle, the good man showed me into the room which Lambert had at that time lived in. I wanted to find some vestiges of his writings, if he should have left any. There among his papers, untouched by the old man from that fine instinct of grief that characterized the aged, I found a number of letters, too illegible ever to have been sent to Mademoiselle de Villenoix. My familiarity with Lambert's writing enabled me in time to decipher the hieroglyphics of this shorthand, the result of impatience and a frenzy of passion. Carried away by his feelings, he had written without being conscious of the irregularity of words too slow to express his thoughts. He must have been compelled to copy these chaotic attempts, for the lines often ran into each other; but he was also afraid perhaps of not having sufficiently disguised his feelings, and at first, at any rate, he had probably written his love-letters twice over.

It required all the fervency of my devotion to his memory, and the sort of fanaticism which comes of such a task, to enable me to divine and restore the meaning of the five letters that here follow. These documents, preserved by me with pious care, are the only material evidence of his overmastering passion. Mademoiselle de Villenoix had no doubt destroyed the real letters that she received, eloquent witnesses to the delirium she inspired.

The first of these papers, evidently a rough sketch, betrays by its style and by its length the many emendations, the heartfelt alarms, the innumerable terrors caused by a desire to please; the changes of expression and the hesitation between the whirl of ideas that beset a man as he indites his first love-letter—a letter he never will forget, each line the result of a reverie, each word the subject of long cogitation, while the most unbridled passion known to man feels the necessity of the most reserved utterance, and like a giant stooping to enter a hovel, speaks humbly and low, so as not to alarm a girl's soul.

No antiquary ever handled his palimpsests with greater respect than I showed in reconstructing these mutilated documents of such joy and suffering as must always be sacred to those who have known similar joy and grief.

I

"Mademoiselle, when you have read this letter, if you ever should read it, my life will be in your hands, for I love you; and to me, the hope of

being loved is life. Others, perhaps, ere now, have, in speaking of themselves, misused the words I must employ to depict the state of my soul; yet, I beseech you to believe in the truth of my expressions; though weak, they are sincere. Perhaps I ought not thus to proclaim my love. Indeed, my heart counseled me to wait in silence till my passion should touch you, that I might the better conceal it if its silent demonstrations should displease you; or till I could express it even more delicately than in words if I found favor in your eyes. However, after having listened for long to the coy fears that fill a youthful heart with alarms, I write in obedience to the instinct which drags useless lamentations from the dying.

"It has needed all my courage to silence the pride of poverty, and to overleap the barriers which prejudice erects between you and me. I have had to smother many reflections to love you in spite of your wealth; and as I write to you, am I not in danger of the scorn which women often reserve for profession of love, which they accept only as one more tribute of flattery? But we cannot help rushing with all our might towards happiness, or being attracted to the life of love as a plant is to the light; we must have been very unhappy before we can conquer the torment, the anguish of those secret deliberations when reason proves to us by a thousand arguments how barren our yearning must be if it remains buried in our hearts, and when hopes bid us dare everything.

"I was happy when I admired you in silence; I was so lost in the contemplation of your beautiful soul, that only to see you left me hardly anything further to imagine. And I should not now have dared to address you if I had not heard that you were leaving. What misery has that one word brought upon me! Indeed, it is my despair that has shown me the extent of my attachment—it is unbounded. Mademoiselle, you will never know—at least, I hope you may never know—the anguish of dreading lest you should lose the only happiness that has dawned on you on earth, the only thing that has thrown a gleam of light in the darkness of misery. I understood yesterday that my life was no more in myself, but in you. There is but one woman in the world for me, as there is but one thought in my soul. I dare not tell you to what a state I am reduced by my love for you. I would have you only as a gift from yourself; I must therefore avoid showing myself to you in all the attractiveness of dejection—for is it not often more impressive to a noble soul than that of good fortune? There are

many things I may not tell you. Indeed, I have too lofty a notion of love to taint it with ideas that are alien to its nature. If my soul is worthy of yours, and my life pure, your heart will have a sympathetic insight, and you will understand me!

"It is the fate of man to offer himself to the woman who can make him believe in happiness; but it is your prerogative to reject the truest passion if it is not in harmony with the vague voices in your heart—that I know. If my lot, as decided by you, must be adverse to my hopes, mademoiselle, let me appeal to the delicacy of your maiden soul and the ingenuous compassion of a woman to burn my letter. On my knees I beseech you to forget all! Do not mock at a feeling that is wholly respectful, and that is too deeply graven on my heart ever to be effaced. Break my heart, but do not rend it! Let the expression of my first love, a pure and youthful love, be lost in your pure and youthful heart! Let it die there as a prayer rises up to die in the bosom of God!

"I owe you much gratitude: I have spent delicious hours occupied in watching you, and giving myself up to the faint dreams of my life; do not crush these long but transient joys by some girlish irony. Be satisfied not to answer me. I shall know how to interpret your silence; you will see me no more. If I must be condemned to know for ever what happiness means, and to be for ever bereft of it; if, like a banished angel, I am to cherish the sense of celestial joys while bound for ever to a world of sorrow —well, I can keep the secret of my love as well as that of my griefs.—And farewell!

"Yes, I resign you to God, to whom I will pray for you, beseeching Him to grant you a happy life; for even if I am driven from your heart, into which I have crept by stealth, still I shall ever be near you. Otherwise, of what value would the sacred words be of this letter, my first and perhaps my last entreaty? If I should ever cease to think of you, to love you whether in happiness or in woe, should I not deserve my punishment?"

II

"You are not going away! And I am loved! I, a poor, insignificant creature! My beloved Pauline, you do not yourself know the power of the look I believe in, the look you gave me to tell me that you had chosen me— you so young and lovely, with the world at your feet!

"To enable you to understand my happiness, I should have to give

you a history of my life. If you had rejected me, all was over for me. I have suffered too much. Yes, my love for you, my comforting and stupendous love, was a last effort of yearning for the happiness my soul strove to reach—a soul crushed by fruitless labor, consumed by fears that make me doubt myself, eaten into by despair which has often urged me to die. No one in the world can conceive of the terrors my fateful imagination inflicts on me. It often bears me up to the sky, and suddenly flings me to earth again from prodigious heights. Deep-seated rushes of power, or some rare and subtle instance of peculiar lucidity, assure me now and then that I am capable of great things. Then I embrace the universe in my mind, I knead, shape it, inform it, I comprehend it —or fancy that I do; then suddenly I awake—alone, sunk in blackest night, helpless and weak; I forget the light I saw but now, I find no succor; above all, there is no heart where I may take refuge.

"This distress of my inner life affects my physical existence. The nature of my character gives me over to the raptures of happiness as defenceless as when the fearful light of reflection comes to analyze and demolish them. Gifted as I am with the melancholy faculty of seeing obstacles and success with equal clearness, according to the mood of the moment, I am happy or miserable by turns.

"Thus, when I first met you, I felt the presence of an angelic nature, I breathed an air that was sweet to my burning breast, I heard in my soul the voice that never can be false, telling me that here was happiness; but perceiving all the barriers that divided us, I understood the vastness of their pettiness, and these difficulties terrified me more than the prospect of happiness could delight me. At once I felt the awful reaction which casts my expansive soul back on itself; the smile you had brought to my lips suddenly turned to a bitter grimace, and I could only strive to keep calm, while my soul was boiling with the turmoil of contradictory emotions. In short, I experienced that gnawing pang to which twenty-three years of suppressed sighs and betrayed affections have not inured me.

"Well, Pauline, the look by which you promised that I should be happy suddenly warmed my vitality, and turned all my sorrows into joy. Now, I could wish that I had suffered more. My love is suddenly full-grown. My soul was a wide territory that lacked the blessing of sunshine, and your eyes have shed light on it. Beloved providence! you will be all in

all to me, orphan as I am, without a relation but my uncle. You will be my whole family, as you are my whole wealth, nay, the whole world to me. Have you not bestowed on me every gladness man can desire in that chaste—lavish—timid glance?

"You have given me incredible self-confidence and audacity. I can dare all things now. I came back to Blois in deep dejection. Five years of study in the heart of Paris had made me look on the world as a prison. I had conceived of vast schemes, and dared not speak of them. Fame seemed to me a prize for charlatans, to which a really noble spirit should not stoop. Thus, my ideas could only make their way by the assistance of a man bold enough to mount the platform of the press, and to harangue loudly the simpletons he scorns. This kind of courage I have not. I ploughed my way on, crushed by the verdict of the crowd, in despair at never making it hear me. I was at once too humble and too lofty! I swallowed my thoughts as other men swallow humiliations. I had even come to despise knowledge, blaming it for yielding no real happiness.

"But since yesterday I am wholly changed. For your sake I now covet every palm of glory, every triumph of success. When I lay my head on your knees, I could wish to attract to you the eyes of the whole world, just as I long to concentrate in my love every idea, every power that is in me. The most splendid celebrity is a possession that genius alone can create. Well, I can, at my will, make for you a bed of laurels. And if the silent ovation paid to science is not all you desire, I have within me the sword of the Word; I could run in the path of honor and ambition where others only crawl.

"Command me, Pauline; I will be whatever you will. My iron will can do anything—I am loved! Armed with that thought, ought not a man to sweep everything before him? The man who wants all can do all. If you are the prize of success, I enter the lists to-morrow. To win such a look as that you bestowed on me, I would leap the deepest abyss. Through you I understand the fabulous achievements of chivalry and the most fantastic tales of the Arabian Nights. I can believe now in the most fantastic excesses of love, and in the success of a prisoner's wildest attempt to recover his liberty. You have aroused the thousand virtues that lay dormant within me—patience, resignation, all the powers of my heart, all the strength of my soul. I live by you and—heavenly thought!—for you.

Everything now has a meaning for me in life. I understand everything, even the vanities of wealth.

"I find myself shedding all the pearls of the Indies at your feet; I fancy you reclining either on the rarest flowers, or on the softest tissues, and all the splendor of the world seems hardly worthy of you, for whom I would I could command the harmony and the light that are given out by the harps of seraphs and the stars of heaven! Alas! a poor, studious poet, I offer you in words treasures I cannot bestow; I can only give you my heart, in which you reign for ever. I have nothing else. But are there no treasures in eternal gratitude, in a smile whose expressions will perpetually vary with perennial happiness, under the constant eagerness of my devotion to guess the wishes of your loving soul? Has not one celestial glance given us assurance of always understanding each other?

"I have a prayer now to be said to God every night—a prayer full of you: 'Let my Pauline be happy!' And will you fill all my days as you now fill my heart?

"Farewell, I can but trust you to God alone!"

III

"Pauline! tell me if I can in any way have displeased you yesterday? Throw off the pride of heart which inflicts on me the secret tortures that can be caused by one we love. Scold me if you will! Since yesterday, a vague, unutterable dread of having offended you pours grief on the life of feeling which you had made so sweet and so rich. The lightest veil that comes between two souls sometimes grows to be a brazen wall. There are no venial crimes in love! If you have the very spirit of that noble sentiment, you must feel all its pangs, and we must be unceasingly careful not to fret each other by some heedless word.

"No doubt, my beloved treasure, if there is any fault, it is in me. I cannot pride myself in the belief that I understand a woman's heart, in all the expansion of its tenderness, all the grace of its devotedness; but I will always endeavor to appreciate the value of what you vouchsafe to show me of the secrets of yours.

"Speak to me! Answer me soon! The melancholy into which we are thrown by the idea of a wrong done is frightful; it casts a shroud over life, and doubts on everything.

"I spent this morning sitting on the bank by the sunken road, gazing at the turrets of Villenoix, not daring to go to our hedge. If you could imagine all I saw in my soul! What gloomy visions passed before me under the gray sky, whose cold sheen added to my dreary mood! I had dark presentiments! I was terrified lest I should fail to make you happy.

"I must tell you everything, my dear Pauline. There are moments when the spirit of vitality seems to abandon me. I feel bereft of all strength. Everything is a burden to me; every fibre of my body is inert, every sense is flaccid, my sight grows dim, my tongue is paralyzed, my imagination is extinct, desire is dead—nothing survives but my mere human vitality. At such times, though you were in all the splendor of your beauty, though you should lavish on me your subtlest smiles and tenderest words, an evil influence would blind me, and distort the most ravishing melody into discordant sounds. At those times—as I believe—some argumentative demon stands before me, showing me the void beneath the most real possessions. This pitiless demon mows down every flower, and mocks at the sweetest feelings, saying: 'Well—and then?' He mars the fairest work by showing me its skeleton, and reveals the mechanism of things while hiding the beautiful results.

"At those terrible moments, when the evil spirit takes possession of me, when the divine light is darkened in my soul without my knowing the cause, I sit in grief and anguish, I wish myself deaf and dumb, I long for death to give me rest. These hours of doubt and uneasiness are perhaps inevitable; at any rate, they teach me not to be proud after the flights which have borne me to the skies where I have gathered a full harvest of thoughts; for it is always after some long excursion in the vast fields of the intellect, and after the most luminous speculations, that I tumble, broken and weary, into this limbo. At such a moment, my angel, a wife would double my love for her—at any rate, she might. If she were capricious, ailing, or depressed, she would need the comforting overflow of ingenious affection, and I should not have a glance to bestow on her. It is my shame, Pauline, to have to tell you that at times I could weep with you, but that nothing could make me smile.

"A woman can always conceal her troubles; for her child, or for the man she loves, she can laugh in the midst of suffering. And could not I, for you, Pauline, imitate the exquisite reserve of a woman? Since yesterday I have doubted my own power. If I could displease you once, if I failed once *to understand you, I dread lest I should often be carried out of our happy circle by my evil demon. Supposing I were to have many of those dreadful moods, or that my unbounded love could not make up for the dark hours of my life—that I were doomed to remain such as I am?—Fatal doubts!*

"Power is indeed a fatal possession if what I feel within me is power. Pauline, go! Leave me, desert me! Sooner would I endure every ill in life than endure the misery of knowing that you were unhappy through me.

"But, perhaps, the demon has had such empire over me only because I have had no gentle, white hands about me to drive him off. No woman has ever shed on me the balm of her affection; and I know not whether, if love should wave his pinions over my head in these moments of exhaustion, new strength might not be given to my spirit. This terrible melancholy is perhaps a result of my isolation, one of the torments of a lonely soul which pays for its hidden treasures with groans and unknown suffering. Those who enjoy little shall suffer little; immense happiness entails unutterable anguish!

"How terrible a doom! If it be so, must we not shudder for ourselves, we who are superhumanly happy? If nature sells us everything at its true value, into what pit are we not fated to fall? Ah! the most fortunate lovers are those who die together in the midst of their youth and love! How sad it all is! Does my soul foresee evil in the future? I examine myself, wondering whether there is anything in me that can cause you a moment's anxiety. I love you too selfishly perhaps? I shall be laying on your beloved head a burden heavy out of all proportion to the joy my love can bring to your heart. If there dwells in me some inexorable power which I must obey—if I am compelled to curse when you pray, if some dark thought coerces me when I would fain kneel at your feet and play as a child, will you not be jealous of that wayward and tricky spirit?

"You understand, dearest heart, that what I dread is not being wholly yours; that I would gladly forego all the sceptres and the palms of the world to enshrine you in one eternal thought, to see a perfect life and an exquisite poem in our rapturous love; to throw my soul into it, drown my powers, and wring from each hour the joys it has to give!

"Ah, my memories of love are crowding back upon me, the clouds of despair will lift. Farewell. I leave you now to be more entirely yours. My beloved soul, I look for a line, a word that may restore my peace of mind. Let me know whether I really grieved my Pauline, or whether some

uncertain expression of her countenance misled me. I could not bear to have to reproach myself after a whole life of happiness, for ever having met you without a smile of love, a honeyed word. To grieve the woman I love—Pauline, I should count it a crime. Tell me the truth, do not put me off with some magnanimous subterfuge, but forgive me without cruelty."

FRAGMENT

"Is so perfect an attachment happiness? Yes, for years of suffering would not pay for an hour of love. "Yesterday, your sadness, as I suppose, passed into my soul as swiftly as a shadow falls. Were you sad or suffering? I was wretched. Whence came my distress? Write to me at once. Why did I not know it? We are not yet completely one in mind. At two leagues' distance or at a thousand I ought to feel your pain and sorrows. I shall not believe that I love you till my life is so bound up with yours that our life is one, till our hearts, our thoughts are one. I must be where you are, see what you feel, feel what you feel, be with you in thought. Did not I know, at once, that your carriage had been overthrown and you were bruised? But on that day I had been with you, I had never left you, I could see you. When my uncle asked me what made me turn so pale, I answered at once, 'Mademoiselle de Villenoix had has a fall.'

"Why, then, yesterday, did I fail to read your soul? Did you wish to hide the cause of your grief? However, I fancied I could feel that you were arguing in my favor, though in vain, with that dreadful Salomon, who freezes my blood. That man is not of our heaven.

"Why do you insist that our happiness, which has no resemblance to that of other people, should conform to the laws of the world? And yet I delight too much in your bashfulness, your religion, your superstitions, not to obey your lightest whim. What you do must be right; nothing can be purer than your mind, as nothing is lovelier than your face, which reflects your divine soul.

"I shall wait for a letter before going along the lanes to meet the sweet hour you grant me. Oh! if you could know how the sight of those turrets makes my heart throb when I see them edged with light by the moon, our only confidante."

"Farewell to glory, farewell to the future, to the life I had dreamed of! Now, my well-beloved, my glory is that I am yours, and worthy of you; my future lies entirely in the hope of seeing you; and is not my life summed up in sitting at your feet, in lying under your eyes, in drawing deep breaths in the heaven you have created for me? All my powers, all my thoughts must be yours, since you could speak those thrilling words, 'Your sufferings must be mine!' Should I not be stealing some joys from love, some moments from happiness, some experiences from your divine spirit, if I gave my hours to study—ideas to the world and poems to the poets? Nay, nay, my very life, I will treasure everything for you; I will bring to you every flower of my soul. Is there anything fine enough, splendid enough, in all the resources of the world, or of intellect, to do honor to a heart so rich, so pure as yours —the heart to which I dare now and again to unite my own? Yes, now and again, I dare believe that I can love as much as you do.

"And yet, no; you are the angel-woman; there will always be a greater charm in the expression of your feelings, more harmony in your voice, more grace in your smile, more purity in your looks than in mine. Let me feel that you are the creature of a higher sphere than that I live in; it will be your pride to have descended from it; mine, that I should have deserved you; and you will not perhaps have fallen too far by coming down to me in my poverty and misery. Nay, if a woman's most glorious refuge is in a heart that is wholly her own, you will always reign supreme in mine. Not a thought, not a deed, shall ever pollute this heart, this glorious sanctuary, so long as you vouchsafe to dwell in it —and will you not dwell in it for ever? Did you not enchant me by the words, 'Now and for ever?' Nunc et semper! And I have written these words of our ritual below your portrait—words worthy of you, as they are of God. He is nunc et semper, as my love is.

"Never, no, never, can I exhaust that which is immense, infinite, unbounded—and such is the feeling I have for you; I have imagined its immeasurable extent, as we measure space by the dimensions of one of its parts. I have had ineffable joys, whole hours filled with delicious meditation, as I have recalled a single gesture or the tone of a word of *yours. Thus there will be memories of which the magnitude will overpower me, if the reminiscence of a sweet and friendly interview is enough to make me shed tears of joy, to move and thrill my soul, and to be an inexhaustible wellspring of gladness. Love is the life of angels!*

"I can never, I believe, exhaust my joy in seeing you. This rapture, the least fervid of any, though it never can last long enough, has made me apprehend the eternal contemplation in which seraphs and spirits abide in the presence of God; nothing can be more natural, if from His essence there emanates a light as fruitful of new emotions as that of your eyes is, of your imposing brow, and your beautiful countenance—the image of your soul. Then, the soul, our second self, whose pure form can never perish, makes our love immortal. I would there were some other language than that I use to express to you the ever-new ecstasy of my love; but since there is one of our own creating, since our looks are living speech, must we not meet face to face to read in each other's eyes those questions and answers from the heart, that are so living, so penetrating, that one evening you could say to me, 'Be silent!' when I was not speaking. Do you remember it, dear life?

"When I am away from you in the darkness of absence, am I not reduced to use human words, too feeble to express heavenly feelings? But words at any rate represent the marks these feelings leave in my soul, just as the word God imperfectly sums up the notions we form of that mysterious First Cause. But, in spite of the subtleties and infinite variety of language, I have no words that can express to you the exquisite union by which my life is merged into yours whenever I think of you.

"And with what word can I conclude when I cease writing to you, and yet do not part from you? What can farewell mean, unless in death? But is death a farewell? Would not my spirit be then more closely one with yours? Ah! my first and last thought; formerly I offered you my heart and life on my knees; now what fresh blossoms of feelings can I discover in my soul that I have not already given you? It would be a gift of a part of what is wholly yours.

"Are you my future? How deeply I regret the past! I would I could have back all the years that are ours no more, and give them to you to reign over, as you do over my present life. What indeed was that time when I knew you not? It would be a void but that I was so wretched."

FRAGMENT

"Beloved angel, how delightful last evening was! How full of riches your dear heart is! And is your love endless, like mine? Each word brought me fresh joy, and each look made it deeper. The placid expression of your countenance gave our thoughts a limitless horizon. It was all as infinite as the sky, and as bland as its blue. The refinement of your adored features repeated itself by some inexplicable magic in your pretty movements and your least gestures. I knew that you were all graciousness, all love, but I did not know how variously graceful you could be. Everything combined to urge me to tender solicitation, to make me ask the first kiss that a woman always refuses, no doubt that it may be snatched from her. You, dear soul of my life, will never guess beforehand what you may grant to my love, and will yield perhaps without knowing it! You are utterly true, and obey your heart alone.

"The sweet tones of your voice blended with the tender harmonies that filled the quiet air, the cloudless sky. Not a bird piped, not a breeze whispered—solitude, you, and I. The motionless leaves did not quiver in the beautiful sunset hues which are both light and shadow. You felt that heavenly poetry—you who experienced so many various emotions, and who so often raised your eyes to heaven to avoid answering me. You who are proud and saucy, humble and masterful, who give yourself to me so completely in spirit and in thought, and evade the most bashful caress. Dear witcheries of the heart! They ring in my ears; they sound and play there still. Sweet words but half spoken, like a child's speech, neither promise nor confession, but allowing love to cherish its fairest hopes without fear or torment! How pure a memory for life! What a free blossoming of all the flowers that spring from the soul, which a mere trifle can blight, but which, at that moment, everything warmed and expanded.

"And it will always be so, will it not, my beloved? As I recall, this morning, the fresh and living delights revealed to me in that hour, I am conscious of a joy which makes me conceive of true love as an ocean of everlasting and ever-new experiences, into which we may plunge with increasing delight. Every day, every word, every kiss, every glance, must increase it by its tribute of past happiness. Hearts that are large enough never to forget must live every moment in their past joys as much as in those promised by the future. This was my dream of old, and now it is no

longer a dream! Have I not met on this earth with an angel who had made me know all its happiness, as a reward, perhaps, for having endured all its torments? Angel of heaven, I salute thee with a kiss.

"I shall send you this hymn of thanksgiving from my heart, I owe it to you; but it can hardly express my gratitude or the morning worship my heart offers up day by day to her who epitomized the whole gospel of the heart in this divine word: 'Believe.'"

V

"What! no further difficulties, dearest heart! We shall be free to belong to each other every day, every hour, every minute, and for ever! We may be as happy for all the days of our life as we now are by stealth, at rare intervals! Our pure, deep feelings will assume the expression of the thousand fond acts I have dreamed of. For me your little foot will be bared, you will be wholly mine! Such happiness kills me; it is too much for me. My head is too weak, it will burst with the vehemence of my ideas. I cry and I laugh—I am possessed! Every joy is an arrow of flame; it pierces and burns me. In fancy you rise before my eyes, ravished and dazzled by numberless and capricious images of delight.

"In short, our whole future life is before me—its torrents, its still places, its joys; it seethes, it flows on, it lies sleeping; then again it awakes fresh and young. I see myself and you side by side, walking with equal pace, living in the same thought; each dwelling in each other's heart, understanding each other, responding to each other as an echo catches and repeats a sound across wide distances.

"Can life be long when it is thus consumed hour by hour? Shall we not die in a first embrace? What if our souls have already met in that sweet evening kiss which almost overpowered us—a feeling kiss, but the crown of my hopes, the ineffectual expression of all the prayers I breathe while we are apart, hidden in my soul like remorse?

"I, who would creep back and hide in the hedge only to hear your footsteps as you went homewards—I may henceforth admire you at my leisure, see you busy, moving, smiling, prattling! An endless joy! You cannot imagine all the gladness it is to me to see you going and coming; only a man can know that deep delight. Your least movement gives me greater pleasure than a mother even can feel as she sees her child asleep or at play. I love you with every kind of love in one. The grace of your least gesture is always new to me. I fancy I could spend whole nights breathing your breath; I would I could steal into every detail of your life, be the very substance of your thoughts—be your very self.

"Well, we shall, at any rate, never part again! No human alloy shall ever disturb our love, infinite in its phases and as pure as all things are which are One—our love, vast as the sea, vast as the sky! You are mine! all mine! I may look into the depths of your eyes to read the sweet soul that alternately hides and shines there, to anticipate your wishes.

"My best-beloved, listen to some things I have never yet dared to tell you, but which I may confess to you now. I felt a certain bashfulness of soul which hindered the full expression of my feelings, so I strove to shroud them under the garbs of thoughts. But now I long to lay my heart bare before you, to tell you of the ardor of my dreams, to reveal the boiling demands of my senses, excited, no doubt, by the solitude in which I have lived, perpetually fired by conceptions of happiness, and aroused by you, so fair in form, so attractive in manner. How can I express to you my thirst for the unknown rapture of possessing an adored wife, a rapture to which the union of two souls by love must give frenzied intensity. Yes, my Pauline, I have sat for hours in a sort of stupor caused by the violence of my passionate yearning, lost in the dream of a caress as though in a bottomless abyss. At such moments my whole vitality, my thoughts and powers, are merged and united in what I must call desire, for lack of a word to express that nameless delirium.

"And I may confess to you now that one day, when I would not take your hand when you offered it so sweetly—an act of melancholy prudence that made you doubt my love—I was in one of those fits of madness when a man could commit a murder to possess a woman.

Yes, if I had felt the exquisite pressure you offered me as vividly as I heard your voice in my heart, I know not to what lengths my passion might not have carried me. But I can be silent, and suffer a great deal. Why speak of this anguish when my visions are to become realities? It will be in my power now to make life one long love-making!

"Dearest love, there is a certain effect of light on your black hair which could rivet me for hours, my eyes full of tears, as I gazed at your sweet person, were it not that you turn away and say, 'For shame; you make me quite shy!'

"To-morrow, then, our love is to be made known! Oh, Pauline! the eyes of others, the curiosity of strangers, weigh on my soul. Let us go to Villenoix, and stay there far from every one. I should like no creature in human form to intrude into the sanctuary where you are to be mine; I could even wish that, when we are dead, it should cease to exist—should be destroyed. Yes, I would fain hide from all nature a happiness which we alone can understand, alone can feel, which is so stupendous that I throw myself into it only to die—it is a gulf!

"Do not be alarmed by the tears that have wetted this page; they are tears of joy. My only blessing, we need never part again!"

In 1823 I traveled from Paris to Touraine by diligence. At Mer we took up a passenger for Blois. As the guard put him into that part of the coach where I had my seat, he said jestingly:

"You will not be crowded, Monsieur Lefebvre!"—I was, in fact, alone.

On hearing this name, and seeing a white-haired old man, who looked eighty at least, I naturally thought of Lambert's uncle. After a few ingenious questions, I discovered that I was not mistaken. The good man had been looking after his vintage at Mer, and was returning to Blois. I then asked for some news of my old "chum." At the first word, the old priest's face, as grave and stern already as that of a soldier who has gone through many hardships, became more sad and dark; the lines on his forehead were slightly knit, he set his lips, and said, with a suspicious glance:

"Then you have never seen him since you left the College?"

"Indeed, I have not," said I. "But we are equally to blame for our forgetfulness. Young men, as you know, lead such an adventurous and storm-tossed life when they leave their school-forms, that it is only by meeting that they can be sure of an enduring affection. However, a reminiscence of youth sometimes comes as a reminder, and it is impossible to forget entirely, especially when two lads have been such friends as we were. We went by the name of the Poet-and-Pythagoras."

I told him my name; when he heard it, the worthy man grew gloomier than ever.

"Then you have not heard his story?" said he. "My poor

nephew was to be married to the richest heiress in Blois; but the day before his wedding he went mad."

"Lambert! Mad!" cried I in dismay. "But from what cause? He had the finest memory, the most strongly-constituted brain, the soundest judgment, I ever met with. Really a great genius—with too great a passion for mysticism perhaps; but the kindest heart in the world. Something most extraordinary must have happened?"

"I see you knew him well," said the priest.

From Mer, till we reached Blois, we talked only of my poor friend, with long digressions, by which I learned the facts I have already related in the order of their interest. I confessed to his uncle the character of our studies and of his nephew's predominant ideas; then the old man told me of the events that had come into Lambert's life since our parting. From Monsieur Lefebvre's account, Lambert had betrayed some symptoms of madness before his marriage; but they were such as are common to men who love passionately, and seemed to me less startling when I knew how vehement his love had been and when I saw Mademoiselle de Villenoix. In the country, where ideas are scarce, a man overflowing with original thought and devoted to a system, as Louis was, might well be regarded as eccentric, to say the least. His language would, no doubt, seem the stranger because he so rarely spoke. He would say, "That man does not dwell in heaven," where any one else would have said, "We are not made on the same pattern." Every clever man has his own quirks of speech. The broader his genius, the more conspicuous are the singularities which constitute the various degrees of eccentricity. In the country an eccentric man is at once set down as half mad.

Hence Monsieur Lefebvre's first sentences left me doubtful of my schoolmate's insanity. I listened to the old man, but I criticised his statements.

The most serious symptom had supervened a day or two before the marriage. Louis had had some well-marked attacks of catalepsy. He had once remained motionless for fifty-nine hours, his eyes staring, neither speaking nor eating; a purely nervous affection, to which persons under the influence of violent passion are liable; a rare malady, but perfectly well known to the medical faculty. What was really extraordinary was that Louis should not have had several previous attacks, since his habits of rapt thought and the character of his mind would predispose him to them. But his temperament, physical and mental, was so admirably balanced, that it had no doubt been able to resist the demands on his strength. The excitement to which he had been wound up by the anticipation of acute physical enjoyment, enhanced by a chaste life and a highly-strung soul, had no doubt led to these attacks, of which the results are as little known as the cause.

The letters that have by chance escaped destruction show very plainly a transition from pure idealism to the most intense sensualism.

Time was when Lambert and I had admired this phenomenon of the human mind, in which he saw the fortuitous separation of our two natures, and the signs of a total removal of the inner man, using its unknown faculties under the operation of an unknown cause. This disorder, a mystery as deep as that of sleep, was connected with the scheme of evidence which Lambert had set forth in his Treatise on the Will. And when Monsieur Lefebvre spoke to me of Louis' first attack, I suddenly remembered a conversation we had had on the subject after reading a medical book.

"Deep meditation and rapt ecstasy are perhaps the undeveloped germs of catalepsy," he said in conclusion.

On the occasion when he so concisely formulated this idea, he had been trying to link mental phenomena together by a series of results, following the processes of the intellect step by step, from their beginnings as those simple, purely animal impulses of instinct, which are all-sufficient to many human beings, particularly to those men whose energies are wholly spent in mere mechanical labor; then, going on to the aggregation of ideas and rising to comparison, reflection, meditation, and finally ecstasy and catalepsy. Lambert, of course, in the artlessness of youth, imagined that he had laid down the lines of a great work when he thus built up a scale of the various degrees of man's mental powers.

I remember that, by one of those chances which seems like predestination, we got hold of a great Martyrology, in which the most curious narratives are given of the total abeyance of physical life which a man can attain to under the paroxysms of the inner life. By reflecting on the effects of fanaticism, Lambert was led to believe that the collected ideas to which we give the name of feelings may very possibly be the material outcome of some fluid which is generated in all men, more or less abundantly, according to the way in which their organs absorb, from the medium in which they live, the elementary atoms that produce it. We went crazy over catalepsy; and with the eagerness that boys throw into every pursuit, we endeavored to endure pain by thinking of something else. We exhausted ourselves by making experiments not unlike those of the epileptic fanatics of the last century, a religious mania which will some day be of service to the science of humanity. I would stand on Lambert's chest, remaining there for several minutes without giving him the slightest pain; but notwithstanding these crazy attempts, we did not achieve an attack of catalepsy.

This digression seemed necessary to account for my first doubts, which were, however, completely dispelled by Monsieur Lefebvre.

"When this attack had passed off," said he, "my nephew sank into a state of extreme terror, a dejection that nothing could overcome. He thought himself unfit for marriage. I watched him with the care of a mother for her child, and found him preparing to perform on himself the operation to which Origen believed he owed his talents. I at once carried him off to Paris, and placed him under the care of Monsieur Esquirol. All through our journey Louis sat sunk in almost unbroken torpor, and did not recognize me. The Paris physicians pronounced him incurable, and unanimously advised his being left in perfect solitude, with nothing to break the silence that was needful for his very improbable recovery, and that he should live always in a cool room with a subdued light.— Mademoiselle de Villenoix, whom I had been careful not to apprise of Louis' state," he went on, blinking his eyes, "but who was supposed to have broken off the match, went to Paris and heard what the doctors had pronounced. She immediately begged to see my nephew, who hardly recognized her; then, like the noble soul she is, she insisted on devoting herself to giving him such care as might tend to his recovery. She would have been obliged to do so if

he had been her husband, she said, and could she do less for him as
her lover?

"She removed Louis to Villenoix, where they have been living
for two years."

So, instead of continuing my journey, I stopped at Blois to go to
see Louis. Good Monsieur Lefebvre would not hear of my lodging
anywhere but at his house, where he showed me his nephew's
room with the books and all else that had belonged to him. At every
turn the old man could not suppress some mournful exclamation,
showing what hopes Louis' precocious genius had raised, and the
terrible grief into which this irreparable ruin had plunged him.

"That young fellow knew everything, my dear sir!" said he,
laying on the table a volume containing Spinoza's works. "How
could so well organized a brain go astray?"

"Indeed, monsieur," said I, "was it not perhaps the result of its
being so highly organized? If he really is a victim to the malady as
yet unstudied in all its aspects, which is known simply as madness,
I am inclined to attribute it to his passion. His studies and his mode
of life had strung his powers and faculties to a degree of energy
beyond which the least further strain was too much for nature;
Love was enough to crack them, or to raise them to a new form of
expression which we are maligning perhaps, by ticketing it without
due knowledge. In fact, he may perhaps have regarded the joys of
marriage as an obstacle to the perfection of his inner man and his
flight towards spiritual spheres."

"My dear sir," said the old man, after listening to me with
attention, "your reasoning is, no doubt, very sound; but even if I
could follow it, would this melancholy logic comfort me for the loss
of my nephew?"

Lambert's uncle was one of those men who live only by their
affections.

I went to Villenoix on the following day. The kind old man
accompanied me to the gates of Blois. When we were out on the
road to Villenoix, he stopped me and said:

"As you may suppose, I do not go there. But do not forget what
I have said; and in Mademoiselle de Villenoix's presence affect not
to perceive that Louis is mad."

He remained standing on the spot where I left him, watching me till I was out of sight.

I made my way to the chateau of Villenoix, not without deep agitation. My thoughts were many at each step on this road, which Louis had so often trodden with a heart full of hopes, a soul spurred on by the myriad darts of love. The shrubs, the trees, the turns of the winding road where little gullies broke the banks on each side, were to me full of strange interest. I tried to enter into the impressions and thoughts of my unhappy friend. Those evening meetings on the edge of the coombe, where his lady-love had been wont to find him, had, no doubt, initiated Mademoiselle de Villenoix into the secrets of that vast and lofty spirit, as I had learned them all some years before.

But the thing that most occupied my mind, and gave to my pilgrimage the interest of intense curiosity, in addition to the almost pious feelings that led me onwards, was that glorious faith of Mademoiselle de Villenoix's which the good priest had told me of. Had she in the course of time been infected with her lover's madness, or had she so completely entered into his soul that she could understand all its thoughts, even the most perplexed? I lost myself in the wonderful problem of feeling, passing the highest inspirations of passion and the most beautiful instances of self-sacrifice. That one should die for the other is an almost vulgar form of devotion. To live faithful to one love is a form of heroism that immortalized Mademoiselle Dupuis. When the great Napoleon and Lord Byron could find successors in the hearts of women they had loved, we may well admire Bolingbroke's widow; but Mademoiselle Dupuis could feed on the memories of many years of happiness, whereas Mademoiselle de Villenoix, having known nothing of love but its first excitement, seemed to me to typify love in its highest expression. If she were herself almost crazy, it was splendid; but if she had understood and entered into his madness, she combined with the beauty of a noble heart a crowning effort of passion worthy to be studied and honored.

When I saw the tall turrets of the chateau, remembering how often poor Lambert must have thrilled at the sight of them, my heart beat anxiously. As I recalled the events of our boyhood, I was almost a sharer in his present life and situation. At last I reached a wide, deserted courtyard, and I went into the hall of the house without meeting a soul. There the sound of my steps brought out an old woman, to whom I gave a letter written to Mademoiselle de Villenoix by Monsieur Lefebvre. In a few minutes this woman returned to bid me enter, and led me to a low room, floored with black-and-white marble; the Venetian shutters were closed, and at the end of the room I dimly saw Louis Lambert.

"Be seated, monsieur," said a gentle voice that went to my heart.

Mademoiselle de Villenoix was at my side before I was aware of her presence, and noiselessly brought me a chair, which at first I would not accept. It was so dark that at first I saw Mademoiselle de Villenoix and Lambert only as two black masses perceived against the gloomy background. I presently sat down under the influence of the feeling that comes over us, almost in spite of ourselves, under the obscure vault of a church. My eyes, full of the bright sunshine, accustomed themselves gradually to this artificial night.

"Monsieur is your old school-friend," she said to Louis.

He made no reply. At last I could see him, and it was one of those spectacles that are stamped on the memory for ever. He was standing, his elbows resting on the cornice of the low wainscot, which threw his body forward, so that it seemed bowed under the weight of his bent head. His hair was as long as a woman's, falling over his shoulders and hanging about his face, giving him a resemblance to the busts of the great men of the time of Louis XIV. His face was perfectly white. He constantly rubbed one leg against the other, with a mechanical action that nothing could have checked, and the incessant friction of the bones made a doleful sound. Near him was a bed of moss on boards.

"He very rarely lies down," said Mademoiselle de Villenoix; "but whenever he does, he sleeps for several days."

Louis stood, as I beheld him, day and night with a fixed gaze, never winking his eyelids as we do. Having asked Mademoiselle de Villenoix whether a little more light would hurt our friend, on her reply I opened the shutters a little way, and could see the expression of Lambert's countenance. Alas! he was wrinkled, white-headed, his eyes dull and lifeless as those of the blind. His features seemed all drawn upwards to the top of his head. I made several attempts to talk to him, but he did not hear me. He was a wreck snatched from the grave, a conquest of life from death—or of death from life!

I stayed for about an hour, sunk in unaccountable dreams, and lost in painful thought. I listened to Mademoiselle de Villenoix, who told me every detail of this life—that of a child in arms.

Suddenly Louis ceased rubbing his legs together, and said slowly:

"The angels are white."

I cannot express the effect produced upon me by this utterance, by the sound of the voice I had loved, whose accents, so painfully expected, had seemed to be lost for ever. My eyes filled with tears in spite of every effort. An involuntary instinct warned me, making me doubt whether Louis had really lost his reason. I was indeed well assured that he neither saw nor heard me; but the sweetness of his tone, which seemed to reveal heavenly happiness, gave his speech an amazing effect. These words, the incomplete revelation of an unknown world, rang in our souls like some glorious distant bells in the depth of a dark night. I was no longer surprised that Mademoiselle de Villenoix considered Lambert to be perfectly sane. The life of the soul had perhaps subdued that of the body. His faithful companion had, no doubt—as I had at that moment—intuitions of that melodious and beautiful existence to which we give the name of Heaven in its highest meaning.

This woman, this angel, always was with him, seated at her embroidery frame; and each time she drew the needle out she gazed at Lambert with sad and tender feeling. Unable to endure this terrible sight—for I could not, like Mademoiselle de Villenoix, read all his secrets—I went out, and she came with me to walk for a few minutes and talk of herself and of Lambert.

"Louis must, no doubt, appear to be mad," said she. "But he is not, if the term mad ought only to be used in speaking of those whose brain is for some unknown cause diseased, and who can show no reason in their actions. Everything in my husband is perfectly balanced. Though he did not actively recognize you, it is not that he did not see you. He has succeeded in detaching himself from his body, and discerns us under some other aspect—what that is, I know not. When he speaks, he utters wondrous things. Only it often happens that he concludes in speech an idea that had its beginning in his mind; or he may begin a sentence and finish it in thought. To other men he seems insane; to me, living as I do in his mind, his ideas are quite lucid. I follow the road his spirit travels; and though I do not know every turning, I can reach the goal with him.

"Which of us has not often known what it is to think of some futile thing and be led on to some serious reflection through the ideas or memories it brings in its train? Not unfrequently, after speaking about some trifle, the simple starting-point of a rapid train of reflections, a thinker may forget or be silent as to the abstract connection of ideas leading to his conclusion, and speak again only to utter the last link in the chain of his meditations.

"Inferior minds, to whom this swift mental vision is a thing unknown, who are ignorant of the spirit's inner workings, laugh at the dreamer; and if he is subject to this kind of obliviousness, regard him as a madman. Louis is always in this state; he soars perpetually through the spaces of thought, traversing them with the swiftness of a swallow; I can follow him in his flight. This is the whole history of his madness. Some day, perhaps, Louis will come back to the life in which we vegetate; but if he breathes the air of heaven before the time when we may be permitted to do so, why should we desire to have him down among us? I am content to hear his heart beat, and all my happiness is to be with him. Is he not wholly mine? In three years, twice at intervals he was himself for a few days; once in Switzerland, where we went, and once in an island off the wilds of Brittany, where we took some sea-baths. I have twice been very happy! I can live on memory."

"But do you write down the things he says?" I asked.

"Why should I?" said she.

I was silent; human knowledge was indeed as nothing in this woman's eyes.

"At those times, when he talked a little," she added, "I think I have recorded some of his phrases, but I left it off; I did not understand him then."

I asked her for them by a look; she understood me. This is what I have been able to preserve from oblivion.

I

Everything here on earth is produced by an ethereal substance which is the common element of various phenomena, known inaccurately as electricity, heat, light, the galvanic fluid, the magnetic fluid, and so forth. The universal distribution of this substance, under various forms, constitutes what is commonly known as Matter.

II

The brain is the alembic to which the Animal conveys what each of its organizations, in proportion to the strength of that vessel, can absorb of that Substance, which returns it transformed into Will. The Will is a fluid inherent in every creature endowed with motion. Hence the innumerable forms assumed by the Animal, the results of its combinations with that Substance. The Animal's instincts are the product of the coercion of the environment in which it develops. Hence its variety.

III

In Man the Will becomes a power peculiar to him, and exceeding in intensity that of any other species.

IV

By constant assimilation, the Will depends on the Substance it meets with again and again in all its transmutations, pervading them by Thought, which is a product peculiar to the human Will, in combination with the modifications of that Substance.

V

The innumerable forms assumed by Thought are the result of the greater or less perfection of the human mechanism.

VI

The Will acts through organs commonly called the five senses, which, in fact, are but one — the faculty of Sight. Feeling and tasting, hearing and smelling, are Sight modified to the transformations of the Substance which Man can absorb in two conditions: untransformed and transformed.

VII

Everything of which the form comes within the cognizance of the one sense of Sight may be reduced to certain simple bodies of which the elements exist in the air, the light, or in the elements of air and light. Sound is a condition of the air; colors are all conditions of light; every smell is a combination of air and light; hence the four aspects of Matter with regard to Man — sound, color, smell, and shape — have the same origin, for the day is not far off when the relationship of the phenomena of air and light will be made clear. Thought, which is allied to Light, is expressed in words which depend on sound. To man, then, everything is derived from the Substance, whose transformations vary only through Number — a certain quantitative dissimilarity, the proportions resulting in the individuals or objects of what are classed as Kingdoms.

VIII

When the Substance is absorbed in sufficient number (or quantity) it makes of man an immensely powerful mechanism, in direct communication with the very element of the Substance, and acting on organic nature in the same way as a large stream when it absorbs the smaller brooks. Volition sets this force in motion independently of the Mind. By its concentration it acquires some of the qualities of the Substance, such as the swiftness of light, the penetrating power of electricity, and the faculty of saturating a body; to which must be added that it apprehends what it can do. Still, there is in man a primordial and overruling phenomenon which defies analysis. Man may be dissected completely; the elements of Will and Mind may perhaps be found; but there still will remain beyond apprehension the x against which I once used to struggle. That x is the Word, the Logos, whose communication burns and consumes those who are not prepared to receive it. The Word is for ever generating the Substance.

IX

Rage, like all our vehement demonstrations, is a current of the human force that acts electrically; its turmoil when liberated acts on persons who are present even though they be neither its cause nor its object. Are there not certain men who by a discharge of Volition can sublimate the essence of the feelings of the masses?

X

Fanaticism and all emotions are living forces. These forces in some beings become rivers that gather in and sweep away everything.

XI

Though Space is, certain faculties have the power of traversing it with such rapidity that it is as though it existed not. From your own bed to the frontiers of the universe there are but two steps: Will and Faith.

XII

Facts are nothing; they do not subsist; all that lives of us is the Idea.

XIII

The realm of Ideas is divided into three spheres: that of Instinct, that of Abstractions, that of Specialism.

97

XIV

The greater part, the weaker part of visible humanity, dwells in the Sphere of Instinct. The Instinctives are born, labor, and die without rising to the second degree of human intelligence, namely Abstraction.

XV

Society begins in the sphere of Abstraction. If Abstraction, as compared with Instinct, is an almost divine power, it is nevertheless incredibly weak as compared with the gift of Specialism, which is the formula of God. Abstraction comprises all nature in a germ, more virtually than a seed contains the whole system of a plant and its fruits. From Abstraction are derived laws, arts, social ideas, and interests. It is the glory and the scourge of the earth: its glory because it has created social life; its scourge because it allows man to evade entering into Specialism, which is one of the paths to the Infinite. Man measures everything by Abstractions: Good and Evil, Virtue and Crime. Its formula of equity is a pair of scales, its justice is blind. God's justice sees: there is all the difference. There must be intermediate Beings, then, dividing the sphere of Instinct from the sphere of Abstractions, in whom the two elements mingle in an infinite variety of proportions. Some have more of one, some more of the other. And there are also some in which the two powers neutralize each other by equality of effect.

XVI

Specialism consists in seeing the things of the material univ and the things of the spiritual universe in all their ramifications original and causative. The greatest human geniuses are those who started from the darkness of Abstraction to attain to the light of Specialism. (Specialism, species, sight; speculation, or seeing everything, and all at once; Speculum, a mirror or means of apprehending a thing by seeing the whole of it.) Jesus had the gift of Specialism; He saw each fact in its root and in its results, in the past where it had its rise, and in the future where it would grow and spread; His sight pierced into the understanding of others. The perfection

98

of the inner eye gives rise to the gift of Specialism. Specialism brings with it Intuition. Intuition is one of the faculties of the Inner Man, of which Specialism is an attribute. Intuition acts by an imperceptible sensation of which he who obeys it is not conscious: for instance, Napoleon instinctively moving from a spot struck immediately afterwards by a cannon ball.

XVII

Between the sphere of Abstraction and that of Specialism, as between those of Abstraction and Instinct, there are beings in whom the attributes of both combine and produce a mixture; these are men of genius.

XVIII

Specialism is necessarily the most perfect expression of man, and he is the link binding the visible world to the higher worlds; he acts, sees, and feels by his inner powers. The man of Abstraction thinks. The man of Instinct acts.

XIX

Hence man has three degrees. That of Instinct, below the average; that of Abstraction, the general average; that of Specialism, above the average. Specialism opens to man his true career; the Infinite dawns on him; he sees what his destiny must be.

XX

There are three worlds—the Natural, the Spiritual, and the Divine. Humanity passes through the Natural world, which is not fixed either in its essence and unfixed in its faculties. The Spiritual world is fixed in its essence and unfixed in its faculties. The Divine world is necessarily a Material worship, a Spiritual worship, and a Divine worship: three forms expressed in action, speech, and prayer, or, in other words, in deed, apprehension, and love. Instinct demands deed; Abstraction is concerned with Ideas; Specialism sees the end, it aspires to God with presentiment or contemplation.

XXI

Hence, perhaps, some day the converse of Et Verbum caro factum est will become the epitome of a new Gospel, which will proclaim that The Flesh shall be made the Word and become the Utterance of God.

XXII

The Resurrection is the work of the Wind of Heaven sweeping over the worlds. The angel borne on the Wind does not say: "Arise, ye dead"; he says, "Arise, ye who live!"

Such are the meditations which I have with great difficulty cast in a form adapted to our understanding. There are some others which Pauline remembered more exactly, wherefore I know not, and which I wrote from her dictation; but they drive the mind to despair when, knowing in what an intellect they originated, we strive to understand them. I will quote a few of them to complete my study of this figure; partly, too, perhaps, because, in these last aphorisms, Lambert's formulas seem to include a larger universe than the former set, which would apply only to zoological evolution. Still, there is a relation between the two fragments, evident to those persons — though they be but few — who love to dive into such intellectual deeps.

I

Everything on earth exists solely by motion and number.

II

Motion is, so to speak, number in action.

III

Motion is the product of a force generated by the Word and by Resistance, which is Matter. But for Resistance, Motion would have had no results; its action would have been infinite. Newton's gravitation is not a law, but an effect of the general law of universal motion.

IV

Motion, acting in proportion to Resistance, produces a result which is Life. As soon as one or the other is the stronger, Life ceases.

V

No portion of Motion is wasted; it always produces number; still, it can be neutralized by disproportionate resistance, as in minerals.

VI

Number, which produces variety of all kinds, also gives rise to Harmony, which, in the highest meaning of the word, is the relation of parts to the whole.

VII

But for Motion, everything would be one and the same. Its products, identical in their essence, differ only by Number, which gives rise to faculties.

VIII

Man looks to faculties; angels look to the Essence.

IX

By giving his body up to elemental action, man can achieve an inner union with the Light.

X

Number is intellectual evidence belonging to man alone; by it he acquires knowledge of the Word.

XI

There is a Number beyond which the impure cannot pass: the Number which is the limit of creation.

XII

The Unit was the starting-point of every product: compounds are derived from it, but the end must be identical with the beginning. Hence this Spiritual formula: the compound Unit, the variable Unit, the fixed Unit.

XIII

The Universe is the Unit in variety. Motion is the means; Number is the result. The end is the return of all things to the Unit, which is God.

XIV

Three and Seven are the two chief Spiritual numbers.

XV

Three is the formula of created worlds. It is the Spiritual Sign of the creation, as it is the Material Sign of dimension. In fact, God has worked by curved lines only: the Straight Line is an attribute of the Infinite; and man, who has the presentiment of the Infinite, reproduces it in his works. Two is the number of generation. Three is the number of Life which includes generation and offspring. Add the sum of four, and you have seven, the formula of Heaven. Above all is God; He is the Unit.

102

After going in to see Louis once more, I took leave of his wife and went home, lost in ideas so adverse to social life that, in spite of a promise to return to Villenoix, I did not go.

The sight of Louis had had some mysteriously sinister influence over me. I was afraid to place myself again in that heavy atmosphere, where ecstasy was contagious. Any man would have felt, as I did, a longing to throw himself into the infinite, just as one soldier after another killed himself in a certain sentry box where one had committed suicide in the camp at Boulogne. It is a known fact that Napoleon was obliged to have the hut burned which had harbored an idea that had become a mortal infection.

Louis' room had perhaps the same fatal effect as that sentry box.

These two facts would then be additional evidence in favor of his theory of the transfusion of Will. I was conscious of strange disturbances, transcending the most fantastic results of taking tea, coffee, or opium, of dreams or of fever—mysterious agents, whose terrible action often sets our brains on fire.

I ought perhaps to have made a separate book of these fragments of thought, intelligible only to certain spirits who have been accustomed to lean over the edge of abysses in the hope of seeing to the bottom. The life of that mighty brain, which split up on every side perhaps, like a too vast empire, would have been set forth in the narrative of this man's visions—a being incomplete for lack of force or of weakness; but I preferred to give an account of my own impressions rather than to compose a more or less poetical romance.

Louis Lambert died at the age of twenty-eight, September 25, 1824, in his true love's arms. He was buried by her desire in an island in the park at Villenoix. His tombstone is a plain stone cross, without name or date. Like a flower that has blossomed on the margin of a precipice, and drops into it, its colors and fragrance all unknown, it was fitting that he too should fall. Like many another misprized soul, he had often yearned to dive haughtily into the void, and abandon there the secrets of his own life.

Mademoiselle de Villenoix would, however, have been quite justified in recording his name on that cross with her own. Since her partner's death, reunion has been her constant, hourly hope. But the vanities of woe are foreign to faithful souls.

Villenoix is falling into ruin. She no longer resides there; to the end, no doubt, that she may the better picture herself there as she used to be. She had said long ago:

"His heart was mine; his genius is with God."

CHATEAU DE SACHE
June-July 1832

GOBSECK

DEDICATION

Among all the pupils of the Oratorian school at Vendome, we are, I think, the only two who have afterwards met in mid-career of a life of letters—we who once were cultivating Philosophy when by rights we should have been minding our De viris. When we met, you were engaged upon your noble works on German philosophy, and I upon this study. So neither of us has missed his vocation; and you, when you see your name here, will feel, no doubt, as much pleasure as he who inscribes his work to you.—Your old schoolfellow.

1840 De Balzac

It was one o'clock in the morning, during the winter of 1829-30, but in the Vicomtesse de Grandlieu's salon two persons stayed on who did not belong to her family circle. A young and good-looking man heard the clock strike, and took his leave. When the courtyard echoed with the sound of a departing carriage, the Vicomtesse looked up, saw that no one was present save her brother and a friend of the family finishing their game of piquet, and went across to her daughter. The girl, standing by the chimney-piece, apparently examining a transparent fire-screen, was listening to the sounds from the courtyard in a way that justified certain maternal fears.

"Camille," said the Vicomtesse, "if you continue to behave to young Comte de Restaud as you have done this evening, you will oblige me to see no more of him here. Listen, child, and if you have any confidence in my love, let me guide you in life. At seventeen one cannot judge of past or future, nor of certain social considerations. I have only one thing to say to you. M. de Restaud has a mother, a mother who would waste millions of francs; a woman of no birth, a Mlle. Goriot; people talked a good deal about her at one time. She behaved so badly to her own father, that she certainly does not deserve to have so good a son. The young Count adores her, and maintains her in her position with dutifulness worthy of all praise, and he is extremely good to his brother and sister.—But however admirable his behavior may be," the Vicomtesse added with a shrewd expression, "so long as his mother lives, any family would take alarm at the idea of intrusting a daughter's fortune and future to young Restaud."

"I overheard a word now and again in your talk with Mlle. de Grandlieu," cried the friend of the family, "and it made me anxious to put in a word of my own.—I have won, M. le Comte," he added, turning to his opponent. "I shall throw you over and go to your niece's assistance."

"See what it is to have an attorney's ears!" exclaimed the Vicomtesse. "My dear Derville, how could you know what I was saying to Camille in a whisper?"

"I knew it from your looks," answered Derville, seating himself in a low chair by the fire.

Camille's uncle went to her side, and Mme. de Grandlieu took up her position on a hearth stool between her daughter and Derville.

"The time has come for telling a story, which should modify your judgment as to Ernest de Restaud's prospects."

"A story?" cried Camille. "Do begin at once, monsieur."

The glance that Derville gave the Vicomtesse told her that this tale was meant for her. The Vicomtesse de Grandlieu, be it said, was one of the greatest ladies in the Faubourg Saint-Germain, by reason of her fortune and her ancient name; and though it may seem improbable that a Paris attorney should speak so familiarly to her, or be so much at home in her house, the fact is nevertheless easily explained.

When Mme. de Grandlieu returned to France with the Royal family, she came to Paris, and at first lived entirely on the pension allowed her out of the Civil List by Louis XVIII.—an intolerable position. The Hotel de Grandlieu had been sold by the Republic. It came to Derville's knowledge that there were flaws in the title, and he thought that it ought to return to the Vicomtesse. He instituted proceedings for nullity of contract, and gained the day. Encouraged by this success, he used legal quibbles to such purpose that he compelled some institution or other to disgorge the Forest of Liceney. Then he won certain lawsuits against the Canal d'Orleans, and recovered a tolerably large amount of property, with which the Emperor had endowed various public institutions. So it fell out that, thanks to the young attorney's skilful management, Mme. de Grandlieu's income reached the sum of some sixty thousand francs, to say nothing of the vast sums returned to her by the law of indemnity. And Derville, a man of high character, well informed, modest, and pleasant in company, became the house-friend of the family.

By his conduct of Mme. de Grandlieu's affairs he had fairly earned the esteem of the Faubourg Saint-Germain, and numbered the best families among his clients; but he did not take advantage of his popularity, as an ambitious man might have done. The

Vicomtesse would have had him sell his practice and enter the magistracy, in which career advancement would have been swift and certain with such influence at his disposal; but he persistently refused all offers. He only went into society to keep up his connections, but he occasionally spent an evening at the Hotel de Grandlieu. It was a very lucky thing for him that his talents had been brought into the light by his devotion to Mme. de Grandlieu, for his practice otherwise might have gone to pieces. Derville had not an attorney's soul. Since Ernest de Restaud had appeared at the Hotel de Grandlieu, and he had noticed that Camille felt attracted to the young man, Derville had been as assiduous in his visits as any dandy of the Chausee-d'Antin newly admitted to the noble Faubourg. At a ball only a few days before, when he happened to stand near Camille, and said, indicating the Count:

"It is a pity that yonder youngster has not two or three million francs, is it not?"

"Is it a pity? I do not think so," the girl answered. "M. de Restaud has plenty of ability; he is well educated, and the Minister, his chief, thinks well of him. He will be a remarkable man, I have no doubt. 'Yonder youngster' will have as much money as he wishes when he comes into power."

"Yes, but suppose that he were rich already?"

"Rich already?" repeated Camille, flushing red. "Why all the girls in the room would be quarreling for him," she said, glancing at the quadrilles.

"And then," retorted the attorney, "Mlle. de Grandlieu might not be the one towards whom his eyes are always turned? That is what that red color means! You like him, do you not? Come, speak out."

Camille suddenly rose to go.

"She loves him," Derville thought.

Since that evening, Camille had been unwontedly attentive to the attorney, who approved of her liking for Ernest de Restaud. Hitherto, although she knew well that her family lay under great obligations to Derville, she had felt respect rather than real friendship for him, their relation was more a matter of politeness than of warmth of feeling; and by her manner, and by the tones of her voice, she had always made him sensible of the distance which socially lay between them. Gratitude is a charge upon the inheritance which the second generation is apt to repudiate.

"This adventure," Derville began after a pause, "brings the one romantic event in my life to my mind. You are laughing already," he went on; "it seems so ridiculous, doesn't it, that an attorney should speak of a romance in his life? But once I was five-and-twenty, like everybody else, and even then I had seen some queer things. I ought to begin at the beginning by telling you about some one whom it is impossible that you should have known. The man in question was a usurer.

"Can you grasp a clear notion of that sallow, wan face of his? I wish the Academie would give me leave to dub such faces the lunar type. It was like silver-gilt, with the gilt rubbed off. His hair was iron-gray, sleek, and carefully combed; his features might have been cast in bronze; Talleyrand himself was not more impassive than this money-lender. A pair of little eyes, yellow as a ferret's, and with scarce an eyelash to them, peered out from under the sheltering peak of a shabby old cap, as if they feared the light. He had the thin lips that you see in Rembrandt's or Metsu's portraits of alchemists and shrunken old men, and a nose so sharp at the tip that it put you in mind of a gimlet. His voice was so low; he always spoke suavely; he never flew into a passion. His age was a problem; it was hard to say whether he had grown old before his time, or whether by economy of youth he had saved enough to last him his life.

"His room, and everything in it, from the green baize of the bureau to the strip of carpet by the bed, was as clean and threadbare as the chilly sanctuary of some elderly spinster who spends her days in rubbing her furniture. In winter time, the live brands of the fire smouldered all day in a bank of ashes; there was never any flame in his grate. He went through his day, from his uprising to his evening coughing-fit, with the regularity of a pendulum, and in some sort was a clockwork man, wound up by a night's slumber. Touch a wood-louse on an excursion across your sheet of paper, and the creature shams death; and in something the same way my acquaintance would stop short in the middle of a sentence, while a cart went by, to save the strain to his voice. Following the example of Fontenelle, he was thrifty of pulse-strokes, and concentrated all human sensibility in the innermost sanctuary of Self.

"His life flowed soundless as the sands of an hour-glass. His victims sometimes flew into a rage and made a great deal of noise, followed by a great silence; so is it in a kitchen after a fowl's neck has been wrung.

"Toward evening this bill of exchange incarnate would assume ordinary human shape, and his metals were metamorphosed into a human heart. When he was satisfied with his day's business, he would rub his hands; his inward glee would escape like smoke through every rift and wrinkle of his face;—in no other way is it possible to give an idea of the mute play of muscle which expressed sensations similar to the soundless laughter of Leather Stocking. Indeed, even in transports of joy, his conversation was confined to monosyllables; he wore the same non-committal countenance.

"This was the neighbor Chance found for me in the house in the Rue de Gres, where I used to live when as yet I was only a second clerk finishing my third year's studies. The house is damp and dark, and boasts no courtyard. All the windows look on the street; the whole dwelling, in claustral fashion, is divided into rooms or cells of equal size, all opening upon a long corridor dimly lit with borrowed lights. The place must have been part of an old convent once. So gloomy was it, that the gaiety of eldest sons forsook them on the stairs before they reached my neighbor's door. He and his house were much alike; even so does the oyster resemble his native rock.

"I was the one creature with whom he had any communication, socially speaking; he would come in to ask for a light, to borrow a book or a newspaper, and of an evening he would allow me to go into his cell, and when he was in the humor we would chat together. These marks of confidence were the results of four years of neighborhood and my own sober conduct. From sheer lack of pence, I was bound to live pretty much as he did. Had he any relations or friends? Was he rich or poor? Nobody could give an answer to these questions. I myself never saw money in his room. Doubtless his capital was safely stowed in the strong rooms of the Bank. He used to collect his bills himself as they fell due, running all over Paris on a pair of shanks as skinny as a stag's. On occasion he would be a martyr to prudence. One day, when he happened to have gold in his pockets, a double napoleon worked its way, somehow or other, out of his fob and fell, and another lodger following him up the stairs picked up the coin and returned it to its owner.

"'That isn't mine!' said he, with a start of surprise. 'Mine indeed! If I were rich, should I live as I do!'

"He made his cup of coffee himself every morning on the cast-iron chafing dish which stood all day in the black angle of the grate; his dinner came in from a cookshop; and our old porter's wife went up at the prescribed hour to set his room in order. Finally, a whimsical chance, in which Sterne would have seen predestination, had named the man Gobseck. When I did business for him later, I came to know that he was about seventy-six years old at the time when we became acquainted. He was born about 1740, in some outlying suburb of Antwerp, of a Dutch father and a Jewish mother, and his name was Jean-Esther Van Gobseck. You remember how all Paris took an interest in that murder case, a woman named La belle Hollandaise? I happened to mention it to my old neighbor, and he answered without the slightest symptom of interest or surprise, 'She is my grandniece.'

"That was the only remark drawn from him by the death of his sole surviving next of kin, his sister's granddaughter. From reports of the case I found that La belle Hollandaise was in fact named Sara Van Gobseck. When I asked by what curious chance his grandniece came to bear his surname, he smiled:

"'The women never marry in our family.'

"Singular creature, he had never cared to find out a single relative among four generations counted on the female side. The thought of his heirs was abhorrent to him; and the idea that his wealth could pass into other hands after his death simply inconceivable.

"He was a child, ten years old, when his mother shipped him off as a cabin boy on a voyage to the Dutch Straits Settlements, and there he knocked about for twenty years. The inscrutable lines on that sallow forehead kept the secret of horrible adventures, sudden panic, unhoped-for luck, romantic cross events, joys that knew no limit, hunger endured and love trampled under foot, fortunes risked, lost, and recovered, life endangered time and time again, and saved, it may be, by one of the rapid, ruthless decisions absolved by necessity. He had known Admiral Simeuse, M. de Lally, M. de Kergarouet, M. d'Estaing, le Bailli de Suffren, M. de Portenduere, Lord Cornwallis, Lord Hastings, Tippoo Sahib's father, Tippoo Sahib himself. The bully who served Mahadaji Sindhia, King of Delhi, and did so much to found the power of the Mahrattas, had had dealings with Gobseck. Long residence at St. Thomas brought him in contact with Victor Hughes and other notorious pirates. In his quest of fortune he had left no stone unturned; witness an attempt to discover the treasure of that tribe of savages so famous in Buenos Ayres and its neighborhood. He had a personal knowledge of the events of the American War of Independence. But if he spoke of the Indies or of America, as he did very rarely with me, and never with anyone else, he seemed to regard it as an indiscretion and to repent of it afterwards. If humanity and sociability are in some sort a religion, Gobseck might be ranked as an infidel; but though I set myself to study him, I must confess, to my shame, that his real nature was impenetrable up to the very last. I even felt doubts at times as to his sex. If all usurers are like this one, I maintain that they belong to the neuter gender.

"Did he adhere to his mother's religion? Did he look on Gentiles as his legitimate prey? Had he turned Roman Catholic, Lutheran, Mahometan, Brahmin, or what not? I never knew anything whatsoever about his religious opinions, and so far as I could see, he was indifferent rather than incredulous.

"One evening I went in to see this man who had turned himself to gold; the usurer, whom his victims (his clients, as he styled them) were wont to call Daddy Gobseck, perhaps ironically, perhaps by way of antiphrasis. He was sitting in his armchair, motionless as a statue, staring fixedly at the mantel-shelf, where he seemed to read the figures of his statements. A lamp, with a pedestal that had once been green, was burning in the room; but so far from taking color

112

from its smoky light, his face seemed to stand out positively paler against the background. He pointed to a chair set for me, but not a word did he say.

"'What thoughts can this being have in his mind?' said I to myself. 'Does he know that a God exists; does he know there are such things as feeling, woman, happiness?' I pitied him as I might have pitied a diseased creature. But, at the same time, I knew quite well that while he had millions of francs at his command, he possessed the world no less in idea—that world which he had explored, ransacked, weighed, appraised, and exploited.

"'Good day, Daddy Gobseck,' I began.

"He turned his face towards me with a slight contraction of his bushy, black eyebrows; this characteristic shade of expression in him meant as much as the most jubilant smile on a Southern face.

"'You look just as gloomy as you did that day when the news came of the failure of that bookseller whose sharpness you admired so much, though you were one of his victims.'

"'One of his victims?' he repeated, with a look of astonishment.

"'Yes. Did you not refuse to accept composition at the meeting of creditors until he undertook privately to pay you your debt in full; and did he not give you bills accepted by the insolvent firm; and then, when he set up in business again, did he not pay you the dividend upon those bills of yours, signed as they were by the bankrupt firm?'

"'He was a sharp one, but I had it out of him.'

"'Then have you some bills to protest? To-day is the 30th, I believe.'

"It was the first time I had spoken to him of money. He looked ironically up at me; then in those bland accents, not unlike the husky tones which the tyro draws from a flute, he answered, 'I am amusing myself.'

"'So you amuse yourself now and again?'

"'Do you imagine that the only poets in the world are those who print their verses?' he asked, with a pitying look and shrug of the shoulders.

"'Poetry in that head!' thought I, for as yet I knew nothing of his life.

"'What life could be as glorious as mine?' he continued, and his eyes lighted up. 'You are young, your mental visions are colored by youthful blood, you see women's faces in the fire, while I see nothing but coals in mine. You have all sorts of beliefs, while I have no beliefs at all. Keep your illusions—if you can. Now I will show you life with the discount taken off. Go wherever you like, or stay at home by the fireside with your wife, there always comes a time when you settle down in a certain groove, the groove is your preference; and then happiness consists in the exercise of your faculties by applying them to realities. Anything more in the way of precept is false. My principles have been various, among various men; I had to change them with every change of latitude. Things that we admire in Europe are punishable in Asia, and a vice in Paris becomes a necessity when you have passed the Azores. There are no such things as hard-and-fast rules; there are only conventions adapted to the climate. Fling a man headlong into one social melting pot after another, and convictions and forms and moral systems become so many meaningless words to him. The one thing that always remains, the one sure instinct that nature has implanted in us, is the instinct of self-interest. If you had lived as long as I have, you would know that there is but one concrete reality invariable enough to be worth caring about, and that is—GOLD. Gold represents every form of human power. I have traveled. I found out that there were either hills or plains everywhere: the plains are monotonous, the hills a weariness; consequently, place may be left out of the question. As to manners; man is man all the world over. The same battle between the poor and the rich is going on everywhere; it is inevitable everywhere; consequently, it is better to exploit than to be exploited. Everywhere you find the man of thews and sinews who toils, and the lymphatic man who torments himself; and pleasures are everywhere the same, for when all sensations are exhausted, all that survives is Vanity—Vanity is the abiding substance of us, the I in us. Vanity is only to be satisfied by gold in floods. Our dreams need time and physical means and painstaking thought before they can be realized. Well, gold contains all things in embryo; gold realizes all things for us.

"'None but fools and invalids can find pleasure in shuffling cards all evening long to find out whether they shall win a few pence at the end. None but driveling idiots could spend time in inquiring into all that is happening around them, whether Madame Such-an-One slept single on her couch or in company, whether she has more blood than lymph, more temperament than virtue. None but the dupes, who fondly imagine that they are useful to their like, can interest themselves in laying down rules for political guidance amid events which neither they nor any one else foresees, nor ever will foresee. None but simpletons can delight in talking about stage players and repeating their sayings; making the daily promenade of a caged animal over a rather larger area; dressing for others, eating for others, priding themselves on a horse or a carriage such as no neighbor can have until three days later. What is all this but Parisian life summed up in a few phrases? Let us find a higher outlook on life than theirs. Happiness consists either in strong emotions which drain our vitality, or in methodical occupation which makes existence like a bit of English machinery, working with the regularity of clockwork. A higher happiness than either consists in a curiosity, styled noble, a wish to learn Nature's secrets, or to attempt by artificial means to imitate Nature to some extent. What is this in two words but Science and Art, or passion or calm?—Ah! well, every human passion wrought up to its highest pitch in the struggle for existence comes to parade itself before me—as I live in calm. As for your scientific curiosity, a kind of wrestling bout in which man is never uppermost, I replace it by an insight into all the springs of action in man and woman. To sum up, the world is mine without effort of mine, and the world has not the slightest hold on me. Listen to this,' he went on, 'I will tell you the history of my morning, and you will divine my pleasures.'

"He got up, pushed the bolt of the door, drew a tapestry curtain across it with a sharp grating sound of the rings on the rod, then he sat down again.

"'This morning,' he said, 'I had only two amounts to collect; the rest of the bills that were due I gave away instead of cash to my customers yesterday. So much saved, you see, for when I discount a bill I always deduct two francs for a hired brougham—expenses of collection. A pretty thing it would be, would it not, if my clients were to set me trudging all over Paris for half-a-dozen francs of discount, when no man is my master, and I only pay seven francs in the shape of taxes?

"'The first bill for a thousand francs was presented by a young fellow, a smart buck with a spangled waistcoat, and an eyeglass, and a tilbury and an English horse, and all the rest of it. The bill bore the signature of one of the prettiest women in Paris, married to a Count, a great landowner. Now, how came that Countess to put her name to a bill of exchange, legally not worth the paper it was written upon, but practically very good business; for these women, poor things, are afraid of the scandal that a protested bill makes in a family, and would give themselves away in payment sooner than fail? I wanted to find out what that bill of exchange really represented. Was it stupidity, imprudence, love or charity?

"'The second bill, bearing the signature "Fanny Malvaut," came to me from a linen-draper on the highway to bankruptcy. Now, no creature who has any credit with a bank comes to me. The first step to my door means that a man is desperately hard up; that the news of his failure will soon come out: and, most of all, it means that he has been everywhere else first. The stag is always at bay when I see him, and a pack of creditors are hard upon his track. The Countess lived in the Rue du Helder, and my Fanny in the Rue Montmartre. How many conjectures I made as I set out this morning! If these two women were not able to pay, they would show me more respect than they would show their own fathers. What tricks and grimaces would not the Countess try for a thousand francs! She would be so nice to me, she would talk to me in that ingratiating tone peculiar to endorsers of bills, she would pour out a torrent of coaxing words, perhaps she would beg and pray, and I...' (here the old man turned his pale eyes upon me)— 'and I not to be moved, inexorable!' he continued. 'I am there as the avenger, the apparition of Remorse. So much for hypotheses. I reached the house.

"'"Madame la Comtesse is asleep," says the maid.

"'"When can I see her?"

"'"At twelve o'clock."

"'"Is Madame la Comtesse ill?"

116

"'"No, sir, but she only came home at three o'clock this morning from a ball."

"'"My name is Gobseck, tell her that I shall call again at twelve o'clock," and I went out, leaving traces of my muddy boots on the carpet which covered the paved staircase. I like to leave mud on a rich man's carpet; it is not petty spite; I like to make them feel a touch of the claws of Necessity. In the Rue Montmartre I thrust open the old gateway of a poor-looking house, and looked into a dark courtyard where the sunlight never shines. The porter's lodge was grimy, the window looked like the sleeve of some shabby wadded gown—greasy, dirty, and full of holes.

"'"Mlle. Fanny Malvaut?"

"'"She has gone out; but if you have come about a bill, the money is waiting for you."

"'"I will look in again," said I.

"'As soon as I knew that the porter had the money for me, I wanted to know what the girl was like; I pictured her as pretty. The rest of the morning I spent in looking at the prints in the shop windows along the boulevard; then, just as it struck twelve, I went through the Countess' ante-chamber.

"'"Madame has just this minute rung for me," said the maid; "I don't think she can see you yet."

"'"I will wait," said I, and sat down in an easy-chair.

"'Venetian shutters were opened, and presently the maid came hurrying back.

"'"Come in, sir."

"'From the sweet tone of the girl's voice, I knew that the mistress could not be ready to pay. What a handsome woman it was that I saw in another moment! She had flung an Indian shawl hastily over her bare shoulders, covering herself with it completely, while it revealed the bare outlines of the form beneath. She wore a loose gown trimmed with snowy ruffles, which told plainly that her laundress' bills amounted to something like two thousand francs in the course of a year. Her dark curls escaped from beneath a bright Indian handkerchief, knotted carelessly about her head after the fashion of Creole women. The bed lay in disorder that told of broken slumber. A painter would have paid money to stay a while to see the scene that I saw. Under the luxurious hanging draperies, the pillow, crushed into the depths of an eider-down quilt, its lace border standing out in contrast against the background of blue silk, bore a vague impress that kindled the imagination. A pair of satin slippers gleamed from the great bear-skin rug spread by the carved mahogany lions at the bed-foot, where she had flung them off in her weariness after the ball. A crumpled gown hung over a chair, the sleeves touching the floor; stockings which a breath would have blown away were twisted about the leg of an easy-chair; while ribbon garters straggled over a settee. A fan of price, half unfolded, glittered on the chimney-piece. Drawers stood open; flowers, diamonds, gloves, a bouquet, a girdle, were littered about. The room was full of vague sweet perfume. And—beneath all the luxury and disorder, beauty and incongruity, I saw Misery crouching in wait for her or for her adorer, Misery rearing its head, for the Countess had begun to feel the edge of those fangs. Her tired face was an epitome of the room strewn with relics of past festival. The scattered gewgaws, pitiable this morning, when gathered together and coherent, had turned heads the night before.

"'What efforts to drink of the Tantalus cup of bliss I could read in these traces of love stricken by the thunderbolt remorse—in this visible presentment of a life of luxury, extravagance, and riot. There were faint red marks on her young face, signs of the fineness of the skin; but her features were coarsened, as it were, and the circles about her eyes were unwontedly dark. Nature nevertheless was so vigorous in her, that these traces of past folly did not spoil her beauty. Her eyes glittered. She looked like some Herodias of da Vinci's (I have dealt in pictures), so magnificently full of life and energy was she; there was nothing starved nor stinted in feature or outline; she awakened desire; it seemed to me that there was some passion in her yet stronger than love. I was taken with her. It was a long while since my heart had throbbed; so I was paid then and there—for I would give a thousand francs for a sensation that should bring me back memories of youth.

"'"Monsieur," she said, finding a chair for me, "will you be so good as to wait?"

"'"Until this time to-morrow, madame," I said, folding up the bill again. "I cannot legally protest this bill any sooner." And within myself I said—"Pay the price of your luxury, pay for your name, pay for your ease, pay for the monopoly which you enjoy! The rich have invented judges and courts of law to secure their goods, and the guillotine—that candle in which so many lie in silk, under silken coverlets, there is remorse, and grinding of teeth beneath a smile, and those fantastical lions' jaws are gaping to set their fangs in your heart."

"'Protest the bill! Can you mean it?" she cried, with her eyes upon me; "could you have so little consideration for me?"

"'If the King himself owed money to me, madame, and did not pay it, I should summons him even sooner than any other debtor."

"'While we were speaking, somebody tapped gently at the door.

"'I cannot see any one," she cried imperiously.

"'But, Anastasie, I particularly wish to speak to you."

"'Not just now, dear," she answered in a milder tone, but with no sign of relenting.

"'What nonsense! You are talking to some one," said the voice, and in came a man who could only be the Count.

"'The Countess gave me a glance. I saw how it was. She was thoroughly in my power. There was a time, when I was young, and might perhaps have been stupid enough not to protest the bill. At Pondicherry, in 1763, I let a woman off, and nicely she paid me out afterwards. I deserved it; what call was there for me to trust her?

"'What does this gentleman want?" asked the Count.

"'I could see that the Countess was trembling from head to foot; the white satin skin of her throat was rough, "turned to goose flesh," to use the familiar expression. As for me, I laughed in myself without moving a muscle.

"'This gentleman is one of my tradesmen," she said.

"'The Count turned his back on me; I drew the bill half out of my pocket. After that inexorable movement, she came over to me and put a diamond into my hands. "Take it," she said, "and be gone."

"'We exchanged values, and I made my bow and went. The

diamond was quite worth twelve hundred francs to me. Out in the courtyard I saw a swarm of flunkeys, brushing out their liveries, waxing their boots, and cleaning sumptuous equipages.

"'"This is what brings these people to me!" said I to myself. "It is to keep up this kind of thing that they steal millions with all due formalities, and betray their country. The great lord, and the little man who apes the great lord, bathes in mud once for all to save himself a splash or two when he goes afoot through the streets."

"'Just then the great gates were opened to admit a cabriolet. It was the same young fellow who had brought the bill to me.

"'"Sir," I said, as he alighted, "here are two hundred francs, which I beg you to return to Mme. la Comtesse, and have the goodness to tell her that I hold the pledge which she deposited with me this morning at her disposition for a week."

"'He took the two hundred francs, and an ironical smile stole over his face; it was as if he had said, "Aha! so she has paid it, has she? ... Faith, so much the better!" I read the Countess' future in his face. That good-looking, fair-haired young gentleman is a heartless gambler; he will ruin himself, ruin her, ruin her husband, ruin the children, eat up their portions, and work more havoc in Parisian salons than a whole battery of howitzers in a regiment.

"'I went back to see Mlle. Fanny in the Rue Montmartre, climbed a very steep, narrow staircase, and reached a two-roomed dwelling on the fifth floor. Everything was as neat as a new ducat. I did not see a speck of dust on the furniture in the first room, where Mlle. Fanny was sitting. Mlle. Fanny herself was a young Parisian girl, quietly dressed, with a delicate fresh face, and a winning look. The arrangement of her neatly brushed chestnut hair in a double curve on her forehead lent a refined expression to blue eyes, clear as crystal. The broad daylight streaming in through the short curtains against the window pane fell with softened light on her girlish face. A pile of shaped pieces of linen told me that she was a sempstress. She looked like a spirit of solitude. When I held out the bill, I remarked that she had not been at home when I called in the morning.

"'"But the money was left with the porter's wife," said she.

"'I pretended not to understand.

""You go out early, mademoiselle, it seems."

""I very seldom leave my room; but when you work all night, you are obliged to take a bath sometimes."

"'I looked at her. A glance told me all about her life. Here was a girl condemned by misfortune to toil, a girl who came of honest farmer folk, for she had still a freckle or two that told of country birth. There was an indefinable atmosphere of goodness about her; I felt as if I were breathing sincerity and frank innocence. It was refreshing to my lungs. Poor innocent child, she had faith in something; there was a crucifix and a sprig or two of green box above her poor little painted wooden bedstead; I felt touched, or somewhat inclined that way. I felt ready to offer to charge no more than twelve per cent, and so give something towards establishing her in a good way of business.

""But maybe she has a little youngster of a cousin," I said to myself, "who would raise money on her signature and sponge on the poor girl."

"'So I went away, keeping my generous impulses well under control; for I have frequently had occasion to observe that when benevolence does no harm to him who gives it, it is the ruin of him who takes. When you came in I was thinking that Fanny Malvaut would make a nice little wife; I was thinking of the contrast between her pure, lonely life and the life of the Countess—she has sunk as low as a bill of exchange already, she will sink to the lowest depths of degradation before she has done!'—I scrutinized him during the deep silence that followed, but in a moment he spoke again. 'Well,' he said, 'do you think that it is nothing to have this power of insight into the deepest recesses of the human heart, to embrace so many lives, to see the naked truth underlying it all? There are no two dramas alike: there are hideous sores, deadly chagrins, love scenes, misery that soon will lie under the ripples of the Seine, young men's joys that lead to the scaffold, the laughter of despair, and sumptuous banquets. Yesterday it was a tragedy. A worthy soul of a father drowned himself because he could not support his family. To-morrow is a comedy; some youngster will try to rehearse the scene of M. Dimanche, brought up to date. You have heard the people extol the eloquence of our latter day preachers; now and again I have wasted my time by going to hear them; they produced a change in my opinions, but in my conduct (as somebody said, I can't recollect his name), in my conduct— never!—Well, well; these good priests and your Mirabeaus and Vergniauds and the rest of them, are mere stammering beginners compared with these orators of mine.

"'Often it is some girl in love, some gray-headed merchant on the verge of bankruptcy, some mother with a son's wrong-doing to conceal, some starving artist, some great man whose influence is on the wane, and, for lack of money, is like to lose the fruit of all his labors—the power of their pleading has made me shudder. Sublime actors such as these play for me, for an audience of one, and they cannot deceive me. I can look into their inmost thoughts, and read them as God reads them. Nothing is hidden from me. Nothing is refused to the holder of the purse-strings to loose and to bind. I am rich enough to buy the consciences of those who control the action of ministers, from their office boys to their mistresses. Is not that power?—I can possess the fairest women, receive their softest caresses; is not that Pleasure? And is not your whole social economy summed up in terms of Power and Pleasure?

"'There are ten of us in Paris, silent, unknown kings, the arbiters of your destinies. What is life but a machine set in motion by money? Know this for certain—methods are always confounded with results; you will never succeed in separating the soul from the senses, spirit from matter. Gold is the spiritual basis of existing society.—The ten of us are bound by the ties of common interest; we meet on certain days of the week at the Cafe Themis near the Pont Neuf, and there, in conclave, we reveal the mysteries of finance. No fortune can deceive us; we are in possession of family secrets in all directions. We keep a kind of Black Book, in which we note the most important bills issued, drafts on public credit, or on banks, or given and taken in the course of business. We are the Casuists of the Paris Bourse, a kind of Inquisition weighing and analyzing the most insignificant actions of every man of any fortune, and our forecasts are infallible. One of us looks out over the judicial world, one over the financial, another surveys the administrative, and yet another the business world. I myself keep an eye on eldest sons, artists, people in the great world, and gamblers—on the most sensational side of Paris. Every one who comes to us lets us into his neighbor's secrets. Thwarted passion and mortified vanity are great babblers. Vice and disappointment and vindictiveness are the best of all detectives. My colleagues, like myself, have enjoyed all things, are sated with all things, and have reached the point when power and money are loved for their own sake.

"'Here,' he said, indicating his bare, chilly room, 'here the most high-mettled gallant, who chafes at a word and draws swords for a syllable elsewhere will entreat with clasped hands. There is no city merchant so proud, no woman so vain of her beauty, no soldier of so bold a spirit, but that they entreat me here, one and all, with tears of rage or anguish in their eyes. Here they kneel—the famous artist, and the man of letters, whose name will go down to posterity. Here, in short' (he lifted his hand to his forehead), 'all the inheritances and all the concerns of all Paris are weighed in the balance. Are you still of the opinion that there are no delights behind the blank mask which so often has amazed you by its impassiveness?' he asked, stretching out that livid face which reeked of money.

"I went back to my room, feeling stupefied. The little, wizened old man had grown great. He had been metamorphosed under my eyes into a strange visionary symbol; he had come to be the power of gold personified. I shrank, shuddering, from life and my kind.

"'Is it really so?' I thought; 'must everything be resolved into gold?'

"I remember that it was long before I slept that night. I saw heaps of gold all about me. My thoughts were full of the lovely Countess; I confess, to my shame, that the vision completely eclipsed another quiet, innocent figure, the figure of the woman who had entered upon a life of toil and obscurity; but on the morrow, through the clouds of slumber, Fanny's sweet face rose before me in all its beauty, and I thought of nothing else."

"Will you take a glass of eau sucree?" asked the Vicomtesse, interrupting Derville.

"I should be glad of it."

"But I can see nothing in this that can touch our concerns," said Mme. de Grandlieu, as she rang the bell.

"Sardanapalus!" cried Derville, flinging out his favorite invocation. "Mademoiselle Camille will be wide awake in a moment if I say that her happiness depended not so long ago upon Daddy Gobseck; but as the old gentleman died at the age of ninety, M. de Restaud will soon be in possession of a handsome fortune. This requires some explanation. As for poor Fanny Malvaut, you know her; she is my wife."

"Poor fellow, he would admit that, with his usual frankness, with a score of people to hear him!" said the Vicomtesse.

"I would proclaim it to the universe," said the attorney.

"Go on, drink your glass, my poor Derville. You will never be anything but the happiest and the best of men."

"I left you in the Rue du Helder," remarked the uncle, raising his face after a gentle doze. "You had gone to see a Countess; what have you done with her?"

"A few days after my conversation with the old Dutchman," Derville continued, "I sent in my thesis, and became first a licentiate in law, and afterwards an advocate. The old miser's opinion of me went up considerably. He consulted me (gratuitously) on all the ticklish bits of business which he undertook when he had made quite sure how he stood, business which would have seemed unsafe to any ordinary practitioner. This man, over whom no one appeared to have the slightest influence, listened to my advice with something like respect. It is true that he always found that it turned out very well.

"At length I became head-clerk in the office where I had worked for three years and then I left the Rue des Gres for rooms in my employer's house. I had my board and lodging and a hundred and fifty francs per month. It was a great day for me!

"When I went to bid the usurer good-bye, he showed no sign of feeling, he was neither cordial nor sorry to lose me, he did not ask me to come to see him, and only gave me one of those glances which seemed in some sort to reveal a power of second-sight.

"By the end of a week my old neighbor came to see me with a

tolerably thorny bit of business, an expropriation, and he continued
to ask for my advice with as much freedom as if he paid for it.

"My principal was a man of pleasure and expensive tastes;
before the second year (1818-1819) was out he had got himself into
difficulties, and was obliged to sell his practice. A professional
connection in those days did not fetch the present exorbitant prices,
and my principal asked a hundred and fifty thousand francs. Now
an active man, of competent knowledge and intelligence, might
hope to pay off the capital in ten years, paying interest and living
respectably in the meantime—if he could command confidence. But
I as the seventh child of a small tradesman at Noyon, I had not a
sou to my name, nor personal knowledge of any capitalist but
Daddy Gobseck. An ambitious idea, and an indefinable glimmer of
hope, put heart into me. To Gobseck I betook myself, and slowly
one evening I made my way to the Rue des Gres. My heart
thumped heavily as I knocked at his door in the gloomy house. I
recollected all the things that he used to tell me, at a time when I
myself was very far from suspecting the violence of the anguish
awaiting those who crossed his threshold. Now it was I who was
about to beg and pray like so many others.

"'Well, no, not that,' I said to myself; 'an honest man must keep
his self-respect wherever he goes. Success is not worth cringing for;
let us show him a front as decided as his own.'

"Daddy Gobseck had taken my room since I left the house, so
as to have no neighbor; he had made a little grated window too in
his door since then, and did not open until he had taken a look at
me and saw who I was.

"'Well,' said he, in his thin, flute notes, 'so your principal is
selling his practice?'

"'How did you know that?' said I; 'he has not spoken of it as
yet except to me.'

"The old man's lips were drawn in puckers, like a curtain, to
either corner of his mouth, as a soundless smile bore a hard glance
company.

"'Nothing else would have brought you here,' he said drily,
after a pause, which I spent in confusion.

"'Listen to me, M. Gobseck,' I began, with such serenity as I could assume before the old man, who gazed at me with steady eyes. There was a clear light burning in them that disconcerted me.

"He made a gesture as if to bid me 'Go on.' 'I know that it is not easy to work on your feelings, so I will not waste my eloquence on the attempt to put my position before you—I am a penniless clerk, with no one to look to but you, and no heart in the world but yours can form a clear idea of my probable future. Let us leave hearts out of the question. Business is business, and business is not carried on with sentimentality like romances. Now to the facts. My principal's practice is worth in his hands about twenty thousand francs per annum; in my hands, I think it would bring in forty thousand. He is willing to sell it for a hundred and fifty thousand francs. And here,' I said, striking my forehead, 'I feel that if you would lend me the purchase-money, I could clear it off in ten years' time.'

"'Come, that is plain speaking,' said Daddy Gobseck, and he held out his hand and grasped mine. 'Nobody since I have been in business has stated the motives of his visit more clearly. Guarantees?' asked he, scanning me from head to foot. 'None to give,' he added after a pause, 'How old are you?'

"'Twenty-five in ten days' time,' said I, 'or I could not open the matter.'

"'Precisely.'

"'Well?'

"'It is possible.'

"'My word, we must be quick about it, or I shall have some one buying over my head.'

"'Bring your certificate of birth round to-morrow morning, and we will talk. I will think it over.'

"'Next morning, at eight o'clock, I stood in the old man's room. He took the document, put on his spectacles, coughed, spat, wrapped himself up in his black greatcoat, and read the whole certificate through from beginning to end. Then he turned it over and over, looked at me, coughed again, fidgeted about in his chair, and said, 'We will try to arrange this bit of business.'

"I trembled.

"'I make fifty per cent on my capital,' he continued, 'sometimes I make a hundred, two hundred, five hundred per cent.'

"I turned pale at the words.

"'But as we are acquaintances, I shall be satisfied to take twelve and a half per cent per—(he hesitated)—'well, yes, from you I would be content to take thirteen per cent per annum. Will that suit you?'

"'Yes,' I answered.

"'But if it is too much, stick up for yourself, Grotius!' (a name he jokingly gave me). 'When I ask you for thirteen per cent, it is all in the way of business; look into it, see if you can pay it; I don't like a man to agree too easily. Is it too much?'

"'No,' said I, 'I will make up for it by working a little harder.'

"'Gad! your clients will pay for it!' said he, looking at me wickedly out of the corner of his eyes.

"'No, by all the devils in hell!' cried I, 'it shall be I who will pay. I would sooner cut my hand off than flay people.'

"'Good-night,' said Daddy Gobseck.

"'Why, fees are all according to scale,' I added.

"'Not for compromises and settlements out of Court, and cases where litigants come to terms,' said he. 'You can send in a bill for thousands of francs, six thousand even at a swoop (it depends on the importance of the case), for conferences with So-and-so, and expenses, and drafts, and memorials, and your jargon. A man must learn to look out for business of this kind. I will recommend you as a most competent, clever attorney. I will send you such a lot of work of this sort that your colleagues will be fit to burst with envy. Werbrust, Palma, and Gigonnet, my cronies, shall hand over their expropriations to you; they have plenty of them, the Lord knows! So you will have two practices—the one you are buying, and the other I will build up for you. You ought almost to pay me fifteen per cent on my loan.'

"'So be it, but no more,' said I, with the firmness which means that a man is determined not to concede another point.

"Daddy Gobseck's face relaxed; he looked pleased with me.

"'I shall pay the money over to your principal myself,' said he, 'so as to establish a lien on the purchase and caution-money.'

"'Oh, anything you like in the way of guarantees.'

"'And besides that, you will give me bills for the amount made payable to a third party (name left blank), fifteen bills of ten thousand francs each.'

"'Well, so long as it is acknowledged in writing that this is a double——'

"'No!' Gobseck broke in upon me. 'No! Why should I trust you any more than you trust me?'

"I kept silence.

"'And furthermore,' he continued, with a sort of good humor, 'you will give me your advice without charging fees as long as I live, will you not?'

"'So be it; so long as there is no outlay.'

"'Precisely,' said he. "Ah, by the by, you will allow me to go to see you?' (Plainly the old man found it not so easy to assume the air of good-humor.)

"'I shall always be glad.'

"'Ah! yes, but it would be very difficult to arrange of a morning. You will have your affairs to attend to, and I have mine.'

"'Then come in the evening.'

"'Oh, no!' he answered briskly, 'you ought to go into society and see your clients, and I myself have my friends at my cafe.'

"'His friends!' thought I to myself.—'Very well,' said I, 'why not come at dinner-time?'

"'That is the time,' said Gobseck, 'after 'Change, at five o'clock. Good, you will see me Wednesdays and Saturdays. We will talk over business like a pair of friends. Aha! I am gay sometimes. Just give me the wing of a partridge and a glass of champagne, and we will have our chat together. I know a great many things that can be told now at this distance of time; I will teach you to know men, and what is more—women!'

"'Oh! a partridge and a glass of champagne if you like.'

"'Don't do anything foolish, or I shall lose my faith in you. And don't set up housekeeping in a grand way. Just one old general servant. I will come and see that you keep your health. I have capital invested in your head, he! he! so I am bound to look after you. There, come round in the evening and bring your principal with you!'

"'Would you mind telling me, if there is no harm in asking, what was the good of my birth certificate in this business?' I asked, when the little old man and I stood on the doorstep.

"Jean-Esther Van Gobseck shrugged his shoulders, smiled maliciously, and said, 'What blockheads youngsters are! Learn, master attorney (for learn you must if you don't mean to be taken in), that integrity and brains in a man under thirty are commodities which can be mortgaged. After that age there is no counting on a man.'

"And with that he shut the door.

"Three months later I was an attorney. Before very long, madame, it was my good fortune to undertake the suit for the recovery of your estates. I won the day, and my name became known. In spite of the exorbitant rate of interest, I paid off Gobseck in less than five years. I married Fanny Malvaut, whom I loved with all my heart. There was a parallel between her life and mine, between our hard work and our luck, which increased the strength of feeling on either side. One of her uncles, a well-to-do farmer, died and left her seventy thousand francs, which helped to clear off the loan. From that day my life has been nothing but happiness and prosperity. Nothing is more utterly uninteresting than a happy man, so let us say no more on that head, and return to the rest of the characters.

"About a year after the purchase of the practice, I was dragged into a bachelor breakfast-party given by one of our number who had lost a bet to a young man greatly in vogue in the fashionable world. M. de Trailles, the flower of the dandyism of that day, enjoyed a prodigious reputation."

"But he is still enjoying it," put in the Comte de Born. "No one wears his clothes with a finer air, nor drives a tandem with a better grace. It is Maxime's gift; he can gamble, eat, and drink more gracefully than any man in the world. He is a judge of horses, hats, and pictures. All the women lose their heads over him. He always spends something like a hundred thousand francs a year, and no creature can discover that he has an acre of land or a single dividend warrant. The typical knight errant of our salons, our boudoirs, our boulevards, an amphibian half-way between a man and a woman—Maxime de Trailles is a singular being, fit for anything, and good for nothing, quite as capable of perpetrating a benefit as of planning a crime; sometimes base, sometimes noble, more often bespattered with mire than besprinkled with blood, knowing more of anxiety than of remorse, more concerned with his digestion than with any mental process, shamming passion, feeling nothing. Maxime de Trailles is a brilliant link between the hulks and the best society; he belongs to the eminently intelligent class from which a Mirabeau, or a Pitt, or a Richelieu springs at times, though it is more wont to produce Counts of Horn, Fouquier-Tinvilles, and Coignards."

"Well," pursued Derville, when he had heard the Vicomtesse's brother to the end, "I had heard a good deal about this individual from poor old Goriot, a client of mine; and I had already been at some pains to avoid the dangerous honor of his acquaintance, for I came across him sometimes in society. Still, my chum was so pressing about this breakfast-party of his that I could not well get out of it, unless I wished to earn a name for squeamishness. Madame, you could hardly imagine what a bachelor's breakfast-party is like. It means superb display and a studied refinement seldom seen; the luxury of a miser when vanity leads him to be sumptuous for a day.

"You are surprised as you enter the room at the neatness of the table, dazzling by reason of its silver and crystal and linen damask. Life is here in full bloom; the young fellows are graceful to behold; they smile and talk in low, demure voices like so many brides; everything about them looks girlish. Two hours later you might take the room for a battlefield after the fight. Broken glasses, serviettes crumpled and torn to rags lie strewn about among the nauseous-looking remnants of food on the dishes. There is an uproar that stuns you, jesting toasts, a fire of witticisms and bad jokes; faces are empurpled, eyes inflamed and expressionless, unintentional confidences tell you the whole truth. Bottles are smashed, and songs trolled out in the height of a diabolical racket; men call each other out, hang on each other's necks, or fall to fisticuffs; the room is full of a horrid, close scent made up of a hundred odors, and noise enough for a hundred voices. No one has any notion of what he is eating or drinking or saying. Some are depressed, others babble, one will turn monomaniac, repeating the same word over and over again like a bell set jangling; another tries to keep the tumult within bounds; the steadiest will propose an orgy. If any one in possession of his faculties should come in, he would think that he had interrupted a Bacchanalian rite.

"It was in the thick of such a chaos that M. de Trailles tried to insinuate himself into my good graces. My head was fairly clear, I was upon my guard. As for him, though he pretended to be decently drunk, he was perfectly cool, and knew very well what he was about. How it was done I do not know, but the upshot of it was that when we left Grignon's rooms about nine o'clock in the evening, M. de Trailles had thoroughly bewitched me. I had given him my promise that I would introduce him the next day to our Papa Gobseck. The words 'honor,' 'virtue,' 'countess,' 'honest woman,' and 'ill-luck' were mingled in his discourse with magical potency, thanks to that golden tongue of his.

"When I awoke next morning, and tried to recollect what I had done the day before, it was with great difficulty that I could make a connected tale from my impressions. At last, it seemed to me that the daughter of one of my clients was in danger of losing her reputation, together with her husband's love and esteem, if she could not get fifty thousand francs together in the course of the morning. There had been gaming debts, and carriage-builders' accounts, money lost to Heaven knows whom. My magician of a boon companion had impressed it upon me that she was rich enough to make good these reverses by a few years of economy. But only now did I begin to guess the reasons of his urgency. I confess, to my shame, that I had not the shadow of a doubt but that it was a matter of importance that Daddy Gobseck should make it up with this dandy. I was dressing when the young gentleman appeared.

"'M. le Comte,' said I, after the usual greetings, 'I fail to see why you should need me to effect an introduction to Van Gobseck, the most civil and smooth-spoken of capitalists. Money will be forthcoming if he has any, or rather, if you can give him adequate security.'

"'Monsieur,' said he, 'it does not enter into my thoughts to force you to do me a service, even though you have passed your word.'

"'Sardanapalus!' said I to myself, 'am I going to let that fellow imagine that I will not keep my word with him?'

"'I had the honor of telling you yesterday,' said he, 'that I had fallen out with Daddy Gobseck most inopportunely; and as there is scarcely another man in Paris who can come down on the nail with a hundred thousand francs, at the end of the month, I begged of you to make my peace with him. But let us say no more about it—'

"M. de Trailles looked at me with civil insult in his expression, and made as if he would take his leave.

"'I am ready to go with you,' said I.

"When we reached the Rue de Gres, my dandy looked about him with a circumspection and uneasiness that set me wondering. His face grew livid, flushed, and yellow, turn and turn about, and by the time that Gobseck's door came in sight the perspiration stood in drops on his forehead. We were just getting out of the cabriolet, when a hackney cab turned into the street. My companion's hawk eye detected a woman in the depths of the vehicle. His face lighted up with a gleam of almost savage joy; he called to a little boy who was passing, and gave him his horse to hold. Then we went up to the old bill discounter.

"'M. Gobseck,' said I, 'I have brought one of my most intimate friends to see you (whom I trust as I would trust the Devil,' I added for the old man's private ear). 'To oblige me you will do your best for him (at the ordinary rate), and pull him out of his difficulty (if it suits your convenience).'

"M. de Trailles made his bow to Gobseck, took a seat, and listened to us with a courtier-like attitude; its charming humility would have touched your heart to see, but my Gobseck sits in his chair by the fireside without moving a muscle, or changing a feature. He looked very like the statue of Voltaire under the peristyle of the Theatre-Francais, as you see it of an evening; he had partly risen as if to bow, and the skull cap that covered the top of his head, and the narrow strip of sallow forehead exhibited, completed his likeness to the man of marble.

"'I have no money to spare except for my own clients,' said he.

"'So you are cross because I may have tried in other quarters to ruin myself?' laughed the Count.

"'Ruin yourself!' repeated Gobseck ironically.

"'Were you about to remark that it is impossible to ruin a man who has nothing?' inquired the dandy. 'Why, I defy you to find a better stock in Paris!' he cried, swinging round on his heels.

"This half-earnest buffoonery produced not the slightest effect upon Gobseck.

"'Am I not on intimate terms with the Ronquerolles, the Marsays, the Franchessinis, the two Vandenesses, the Ajuda-Pintos,—all the most fashionable young men in Paris, in short? A prince and an ambassador (you know them both) are my partners at play. I draw my revenues from London and Carlsbad and Baden and Bath. Is not this the most brilliant of all industries!'

"'True.'

"'You make a sponge of me, begad! you do. You encourage me to go and swell myself out in society, so that you can squeeze me when I am hard up; but you yourselves are sponges, just as I am, and death will give you a squeeze some day.'

"'That is possible.'

"'If there were no spendthrifts, what would become of you? The pair of us are like soul and body.'

"'Precisely so.'

"'Come, now, give us your hand, Grandaddy Gobseck, and be magnanimous if this is "true" and "possible" and "precisely so."'

"'You come to me,' the usurer answered coldly, 'because Girard, Palma, Werbrust, and Gigonnet are full up of your paper; they are offering it at a loss of fifty per cent; and as it is likely they only gave you half the figure on the face of the bills, they are not worth five-and-twenty per cent of their supposed value. I am your most obedient! Can I in common decency lend a stiver to a man who owes thirty thousand francs, and has not one farthing?' Gobseck continued. 'The day before yesterday you lost ten thousand francs at a ball at the Baron de Nucingen's.'

"'Sir,' said the Count, with rare impudence, 'my affairs are no concern of yours,' and he looked the old man up and down. 'A man has no debts till payment is due.'

"'True.'

"'My bills will be duly met.'

"'That is possible.'

"'And at this moment the question between you and me is simply whether the security I am going to offer is sufficient for the sum I have come to borrow.'

"'Precisely.'

"A cab stopped at the door, and the sound of wheels filled the room.

"'I will bring something directly which perhaps will satisfy you,' cried the young man, and he left the room.

"'Oh! my son,' exclaimed Gobseck, rising to his feet, and stretching out his arms to me, 'if he has good security, you have saved my life. It would be the death of me. Werbrust and Gigonnet imagined that they were going to play off a trick on me; and now, thanks to you, I shall have a good laugh at their expense to-night.'

"There was something frightful about the old man's ecstasy. It was the one occasion when he opened his heart to me; and that flash of joy, swift though it was, will never be effaced from my memory.

"'Favor me so far as to stay here,' he added. 'I am armed, and a sure shot. I have gone tiger-hunting, and fought on the deck when there was nothing for it but to win or die; but I don't care to trust yonder elegant scoundrel.'

"He sat down again in his armchair before his bureau, and his face grew pale and impassive as before.

"'Ah!' he continued, turning to me, 'you will see that lovely creature I once told you about; I can hear a fine lady's step in the corridor; it is she, no doubt;' and, as a matter of fact, the young man came in with a woman on his arm. I recognized the Countess, whose levee Gobseck had described for me, one of old Goriot's two daughters.

"The Countess did not see me at first; I stayed where I was in the window bay, with my face against the pane; but I saw her give

Maxime a suspicious glance as she came into the money-lender's damp, dark room. So beautiful she was, that in spite of her faults I felt sorry for her. There was a terrible storm of anguish in her heart; her haughty, proud features were drawn and distorted with pain which she strove in vain to disguise. The young man had come to be her evil genius. I admired Gobseck, whose perspicacity had foreseen their future four years ago at the first bill which she endorsed.

"'Probably,' said I to myself, 'this monster with the angel face controls every possible spring of action in her: rules her through vanity, jealousy, pleasure, and the current of life in the world.'"

The Vicomtesse de Grandlieu broke in on the story.

"Why, the woman's very virtues have been turned against her," she exclaimed. "He has made her shed tears of devotion, and then abused her kindness and made her pay very dearly for unhallowed bliss."

Derville did not understand the signs which Mme. de Grandlieu made to him.

"I confess," he said, "that I had no inclination to shed tears over the lot of this unhappy creature, so brilliant in society, so repulsive to eyes that could read her heart; I shuddered rather at the sight of her murderer, a young angel with such a clear brow, such red lips and white teeth, such a winning smile. There they stood before their judge, he scrutinizing them much as some fifteenth-century Dominican inquisitor might have peered into the dungeons of the Holy Office while the torture was administered to two Moors.

"The Countess spoke tremulously. 'Sir,' she said, 'is there any way of obtaining the value of these diamonds, and of keeping the right of repurchase?' She held out a jewel-case.

"'Yes, madame,' I put in, and came forwards.

"She looked at me, and a shudder ran through her as she recognized me, and gave me the glance which means, 'Say nothing of this,' all the world over.

"'This,' said I, 'constitutes a sale with faculty of redemption, as it is called, a formal agreement to transfer and deliver over a piece of property, either real estate or personalty, for a given time, on the expiry of which the previous owner recovers his title to the property in question, upon payment of a stipulated sum.'

"She breathed more freely. The Count looked black; he had grave doubts whether Gobseck would lend very much on the diamonds after such a fall in their value. Gobseck, impassive as ever, had taken up his magnifying glass, and was quietly scrutinizing the jewels. If I were to live for a hundred years, I should never forget the sight of his face at that moment. There was a flush in his pale cheeks; his eyes seemed to have caught the sparkle of the stones, for there was an unnatural glitter in them. He rose and went to the light, holding the diamonds close to his toothless mouth, as if he meant to devour them; mumbling vague words over them, holding up bracelets, sprays, necklaces, and tiaras one after another, to judge their water, whiteness, and cutting; taking them out of the jewel-case and putting them in again, letting the play of the light bring out all their fires. He was more like a child than an old man; or, rather, childhood and dotage seemed to meet in him.

"'Fine stones! The set would have fetched three hundred thousand francs before the Revolution. What water! Genuine Asiatic diamonds from Golconda or Visapur. Do you know what they are worth? No, no; no one in Paris but Gobseck can appreciate them. In the time of the Empire such a set would have cost another two hundred thousand francs!'

"He gave a disgusted shrug, and added:

"'But now diamonds are going down in value every day. The Brazilians have swamped the market with them since the Peace; but the Indian stones are a better color. Others wear them now besides court ladies. Does madame go to court?'

"While he flung out these terrible words, he examined one stone after another with delight which no words can describe.

"'Flawless!' he said. 'Here is a speck!... here is a flaw!... A fine stone that!'

"His haggard face was so lighted up by the sparkling jewels, that it put me in mind of a dingy old mirror, such as you see in country inns. The glass receives every luminous image without reflecting the light, and a traveler bold enough to look for his face in it beholds a man in an apoplectic fit.

"'Well?' asked the Count, clapping Gobseck on the shoulder.

"The old boy trembled. He put down his playthings on his bureau, took his seat, and was a money-lender once more—hard, cold, and polished as a marble column.

"'How much do you want?'

"'One hundred thousand francs for three years,' said the Count.

"'That is possible,' said Gobseck, and then from a mahogany box (Gobseck's jewel-case) he drew out a faultlessly adjusted pair of scales!

"He weighed the diamonds, calculating the value of stones and setting at sight (Heaven knows how!), delight and severity struggling in the expression of his face the meanwhile. The Countess had plunged in a kind of stupor; to me, watching her, it seemed that she was fathoming the depths of the abyss into which she had fallen. There was remorse still left in that woman's soul. Perhaps a hand held out in human charity might save her. I would try.

"'Are the diamonds your personal property, madame?' I asked in a clear voice.

"'Yes, monsieur,' she said, looking at me with proud eyes.

"'Make out the deed of purchase with power of redemption, chatterbox,' said Gobseck to me, resigning his chair at the bureau in my favor.

"'Madame is without doubt a married woman?' I tried again.

"She nodded abruptly.

"'Then I will not draw up the deed,' said I.

"'And why not?' asked Gobseck.

"'Why not?' echoed I, as I drew the old man into the bay window so as to speak aside with him. 'Why not? This woman is under her husband's control; the agreement would be void in law; you could not possibly assert your ignorance of a fact recorded on the very face of the document itself. You would be compelled at once to produce the diamonds deposited with you, according to the weight, value, and cutting therein described.'

"Gobseck cut me short with a nod, and turned towards the guilty couple.

"'He is right!' he said. 'That puts the whole thing in a different light. Eighty thousand francs down, and you leave the diamonds with me,' he added, in the husky, flute-like voice. 'In the way of property, possession is as good as a title.'

"'But——' objected the young man.

"'You can take it or leave it,' continued Gobseck, returning the jewel-case to the lady as he spoke.

"'I have too many risks to run.'

"'It would be better to throw yourself at your husband's feet,' I bent to whisper in her ear.

"The usurer doubtless knew what I was saying from the movement of my lips. He gave me a cool glance. The Count's face grew livid. The Countess was visibly wavering. Maxime stepped up to her, and, low as he spoke, I could catch the words:

"'Adieu, dear Anastasie, may you be happy! As for me, by to-morrow my troubles will be over.'

"'Sir!' cried the lady, turning to Gobseck. 'I accept your offer.'

"'Come, now,' returned Gobseck. 'You have been a long time in coming to it, my fair lady.'

"He wrote out a cheque for fifty thousand francs on the Bank of France, and handed it to the Countess.

"'Now,' continued he with a smile, such a smile as you will see in portraits of M. Voltaire, 'now I will give you the rest of the amount in bills, thirty thousand francs' worth of paper as good as bullion. This gentleman here has just said, "My bills will be met when they are due,"' added he, producing certain drafts bearing the Count's signature, all protested the day before at the request of some of the confraternity, who had probably made them over to him (Gobseck) at a considerably reduced figure.

"The young man growled out something, in which the words 'Old scoundrel!' were audible. Daddy Gobseck did not move an eyebrow. He drew a pair of pistols out of a pigeon-hole, remarking coolly:

"'As the insulted man, I fire first.'

"'Maxime, you owe this gentleman an explanation,' cried the trembling Countess in a low voice.

"'I had no intention of giving offence,' stammered Maxime.

"'I am quite sure of that,' Gobseck answered calmly; 'you had no intention of meeting your bills, that was all.'

"The Countess rose, bowed, and vanished, with a great dread gnawing her, I doubt not. M. de Trailles was bound to follow, but before he went he managed to say:

"'If either of you gentlemen should forget himself, I will have his blood, or he will have mine.'

"'Amen!' called Daddy Gobseck as he put his pistols back in their place; 'but a man must have blood in his veins though before he can risk it, my son, and you have nothing but mud in yours.'

"When the door was closed, and the two vehicles had gone, Gobseck rose to his feet and began to prance about.

"'I have the diamonds! I have the diamonds!' he cried again and again, 'the beautiful diamonds! such diamonds! and tolerably cheaply. Aha! aha! Werbrust and Gigonnet, you thought you had old Papa Gobseck! Ego sum papa! I am master of the lot of you! Paid! paid, principal and interest! How silly they will look to-night when I shall come out with this story between two games of dominoes!'

"The dark glee, the savage ferocity aroused by the possession of a few water-white pebbles, set me shuddering. I was dumb with amazement.

"'Aha! There you are, my boy!' said he. 'We will dine together. We will have some fun at your place, for I haven't a home of my own, and these restaurants, with their broths, and sauces, and wines, would poison the Devil himself.'

"Something in my face suddenly brought back the usual cold, impassive expression to his.

"'You don't understand it,' he said, and sitting down by the hearth, he put a tin saucepan full of milk on the brazier.—'Will you breakfast with me?' continued he. 'Perhaps there will be enough here for two.'

"'Thanks,' said I, 'I do not breakfast till noon.'

"I had scarcely spoken before hurried footsteps sounded from the passage. The stranger stopped at Gobseck's door and rapped; there was that in the knock which suggested a man transported with rage. Gobseck reconnoitred him through the grating; then he opened the door, and in came a man of thirty-five or so, judged harmless apparently in spite of his anger. The newcomer, who was quite plainly dressed, bore a strong resemblance to the late Duc de Richelieu. You must often have met him, he was the Countess' husband, a man with the aristocratic figure (permit the expression to pass) peculiar to statesmen of your faubourg.

"'Sir,' said this person, addressing himself to Gobseck, who had quite recovered his tranquillity, 'did my wife go out of this house just now?'

"'That is possible.'

"'Well, sir? do you not take my meaning?'

"'I have not the honor of the acquaintance of my lady your wife,' returned Gobseck. 'I have had a good many visitors this morning, women and men, and mannish young ladies, and young gentlemen who look like young ladies. I should find it very hard to say——'

"'A truce to jesting, sir! I mean the woman who has this moment gone out from you.'

"'How can I know whether she is your wife or not? I never had the pleasure of seeing you before.'

"'You are mistaken, M. Gobseck,' said the Count, with profound irony in his voice. 'We have met before, one morning in my wife's bedroom. You had come to demand payment for a bill— no bill of hers.'

"'It was no business of mine to inquire what value she had received for it,' said Gobseck, with a malignant look at the Count. 'I had come by the bill in the way of business. At the same time, monsieur,' continued Gobseck, quietly pouring coffee into his bowl of milk, without a trace of excitement or hurry in his voice, 'you will permit me to observe that your right to enter my house and expostulate with me is far from proven to my mind. I came of age in the sixty-first year of the preceding century.'

"'Sir,' said the Count, 'you have just bought family diamonds, which do not belong to my wife, for a mere trifle.'

"'Without feeling it incumbent upon me to tell you my private affairs, I will tell you this much M. le Comte—if Mme. la Comtesse has taken your diamonds, you should have sent a circular around to all the jewelers, giving them notice not to buy them; she might have sold them separately.'

"'You know my wife, sir!' roared the Count.

"'True.'

"'She is in her husband's power.'

"'That is possible.'

"'She had no right to dispose of those diamonds——'

"'Precisely.'

"'Very well, sir?'

"'Very well, sir. I knew your wife, and she is in her husband's power; I am quite willing, she is in the power of a good many people; but—I—do—not—know—your diamonds. If Mme. la Comtesse can put her name to a bill, she can go into business, of course, and buy and sell diamonds on her own account. The thing is plain on the face of it!'

"'Good-day, sir!' cried the Count, now white with rage. 'There are courts of justice.'

"'Quite so.'

"'This gentleman here,' he added, indicating me, 'was a witness of the sale.'

"'That is possible.'

"The Count turned to go. Feeling the gravity of the affair, I suddenly put in between the two belligerents.

"'M. le Comte,' said I, 'you are right, and M. Gobseck is by no means in the wrong. You could not prosecute the purchaser without bringing your wife into court, and the whole of the odium would not fall on her. I am an attorney, and I owe it to myself, and still more to my professional position, to declare that the diamonds of which you speak were purchased by M. Gobseck in my presence; but, in my opinion, it would be unwise to dispute the legality of the sale, especially as the goods are not readily recognizable. In equity our contention would lie, in law it would collapse. M. Gobseck is too honest a man to deny that the sale was a profitable transaction, more especially as my conscience, no less than my duty, compels me to make the admission. But once bring the case into a court of law, M. le Comte, the issue would be doubtful. My advice to you is to come to terms with M. Gobseck, who can plead that he bought the diamonds in all good faith; you would be bound in any case to return the purchase money. Consent to an arrangement, with power to redeem at the end of seven or eight months, or a year even, or any convenient lapse of time, for the repayment of the sum borrowed by Mme. la Comtesse, unless you would prefer to repurchase them outright and give security for repayment.'

"Gobseck dipped his bread into the bowl of coffee, and ate with perfect indifference; but at the words 'come to terms,' he looked at me as who should say, 'A fine fellow that! he has learned something from my lessons!' And I, for my part, riposted with a glance, which he understood uncommonly well. The business was dubious and shady; there was pressing need of coming to terms. Gobseck could not deny all knowledge of it, for I should appear as a witness. The Count thanked me with a smile of good-will.

"In the debate which followed, Gobseck showed greed enough and skill enough to baffle a whole congress of diplomatists; but in the end I drew up an instrument, in which the Count acknowledged the receipt of eighty-five thousand francs, interest included, in consideration of which Gobseck undertook to return the diamonds to the Count.

"'What waste!' exclaimed he as he put his signature to the agreement. 'How is it possible to bridge such a gulf?'

"'Have you many children, sir?' Gobseck asked gravely.

"The Count winced at the question; it was as if the old money-lender, like an experienced physician, had put his finger at once on the sore spot. The Comtesse's husband did not reply.

"'Well,' said Gobseck, taking the pained silence for answer, 'I know your story by heart. The woman is a fiend, but perhaps you love her still; I can well believe it; she made an impression on me. Perhaps, too, you would rather save your fortune, and keep it for one or two of your children? Well, fling yourself into the whirlpool of society, lose that fortune at play, come to Gobseck pretty often. The world will say that I am a Jew, a Tartar, a usurer, a pirate, will say that I have ruined you! I snap my fingers at them! If anybody insults me, I lay my man out; nobody is a surer shot nor handles a rapier better than your servant. And every one knows it. Then, have a friend—if you can find one—and make over your property to him by a fictitious sale. You call that a fidei commissum, don't you?' he asked, turning to me.

"The Count seemed to be entirely absorbed in his own thoughts.

"'You shall have your money to-morrow,' he said, 'have the diamonds in readiness,' and he went.

"'There goes one who looks to me to be as stupid as an honest man,' Gobseck said coolly when the Count had gone.

"'Say rather stupid as a man of passionate nature.'

"'The Count owes you your fee for drawing up the agreement!' Gobseck called after me as I took my leave."

"One morning, a few days after the scene which initiated me into the terrible depths beneath the surface of the life of a woman of fashion, the Count came into my private office.

"'I have come to consult you on a matter of grave moment,' he said, 'and I begin by telling you that I have perfect confidence in you, as I hope to prove to you. Your behavior to Mme. de Grandlieu is above all praise,' the Count went on. (You see, madame, that you have paid me a thousand times over for a very simple matter.)

"I bowed respectfully, and replied that I had done nothing but the duty of an honest man.

"'Well,' the Count went on, 'I have made a great many inquiries about the singular personage to whom you owe your position. And from all that I can learn, Gobseck is a philosopher of the Cynic school. What do you think of his probity?'

"'M. le Comte,' said I, 'Gobseck is my benefactor—at fifteen per cent,' I added, laughing. 'But his avarice does not authorize me to paint him to the life for a stranger's benefit.'

"'Speak out, sir. Your frankness cannot injure Gobseck or yourself. I do not expect to find an angel in a pawnbroker.'

"'Daddy Gobseck,' I began, 'is intimately convinced of the truth of the principle which he takes for a rule of life. In his opinion, money is a commodity which you may sell cheap or dear, according to circumstances, with a clear conscience. A capitalist, by charging a high rate of interest, becomes in his eyes a secured partner by anticipation. Apart from the peculiar philosophical views of human nature and financial principles, which enable him to behave like a usurer, I am fully persuaded that, out of his business, he is the most loyal and upright soul in Paris. There are two men in him; he is petty and great—a miser and a philosopher. If I were to die and leave a family behind me, he would be the guardian whom I should appoint. This was how I came to see Gobseck in this light, monsieur. I know nothing of his past life. He may have been a pirate, may, for anything I know, have been all over the world, trafficking in diamonds, or men, or women, or State secrets; but this I affirm of him—never has human soul been more thoroughly tempered and tried. When I paid off my loan, I asked him, with a little circumlocution of course, how it was that he had made me pay such an exorbitant rate of interest; and why, seeing that I was a friend, and he meant to do me a kindness, he should not have yielded to the wish and made it complete.—"My son," he said, "I released you from all need to feel any gratitude by giving you ground for the belief that you owed me nothing."—So we are the best friends in the world. That answer, monsieur, gives you the man better than any amount of description.'

"'I have made up my mind once and for all,' said the Count. 'Draw up the necessary papers; I am going to transfer my property to Gobseck. I have no one but you to trust to in the draft of the counter-deed, which will declare that this transfer is a simulated sale, and that Gobseck as trustee will administer my estate (as he knows how to administer), and undertakes to make over my fortune to my eldest son when he comes of age. Now, sir, this I must tell you: I should be afraid to have that precious document in my own keeping. My boy is so fond of his mother, that I cannot trust him with it. So dare I beg of you to keep it for me? In case of death, Gobseck would make you legatee of my property. Every contingency is provided for.'

"The Count paused for a moment. He seemed greatly agitated.

"'A thousand pardons,' he said at length; 'I am in great pain, and have very grave misgivings as to my health. Recent troubles have disturbed me very painfully, and forced me to take this great step.'

"'Allow me first to thank you, monsieur,' said I, 'for the trust you place me in. But I am bound to deserve it by pointing out to you that you are disinheriting your—other children. They bear your name. Merely as the children of a once-loved wife, now fallen from her position, they have a claim to an assured existence. I tell you plainly that I cannot accept the trust with which you propose to honor me unless their future is secured.'

"The Count trembled violently at the words, and tears came into his eyes as he grasped my hand, saying, 'I did not know my man thoroughly. You have made me both glad and sorry. We will make provision for the children in the counter-deed.'

"I went with him to the door; it seemed to me that there was a glow of satisfaction in his face at the thought of this act of justice.

"Now, Camille, this is how a young wife takes the first step to the brink of a precipice. A quadrille, a ballad, a picnic party is sometimes cause sufficient of frightful evils. You are hurried on by the presumptuous voice of vanity and pride, on the faith of a smile, or through giddiness and folly! Shame and misery and remorse are three Furies awaiting every woman the moment she oversteps the limits——"

"Poor Camille can hardly keep awake," the Vicomtesse hastily broke in.—"Go to bed, child; you have no need of appalling pictures to keep you pure in heart and conduct."

Camille de Grandlieu took the hint and went.

"You were going rather too far, dear M. Derville," said the Vicomtesse, "an attorney is not a mother of daughters nor yet a preacher."

"But any newspaper is a thousand times——"

"Poor Derville!" exclaimed the Vicomtesse, "what has come over you? Do you really imagine that I allow a daughter of mine to read the newspapers?—Go on," she added after a pause.

"Three months after everything was signed and sealed between the Count and Gobseck——"

"You can call him the Comte de Restaud, now that Camille is not here," said the Vicomtesse.

"So be it! Well, time went by, and I saw nothing of the counter-deed, which by rights should have been in my hands. An attorney in Paris lives in such a whirl of business that with certain exceptions which we make for ourselves, we have not the time to give each individual client the amount of interest which he himself takes in his affairs. Still, one day when Gobseck came to dine with me, I asked him as we left the table if he knew how it was that I had heard no more of M. de Restaud.

"'There are excellent reasons for that,' he said; 'the noble Count is at death's door. He is one of the soft stamp that cannot learn how to put an end to chagrin, and allow it to wear them out instead. Life is a craft, a profession; every man must take the trouble to learn that business. When he has learned what life is by dint of painful experiences, the fibre of him is toughened, and acquires a certain elasticity, so that he has his sensibilities under his own control; he disciplines himself till his nerves are like steel springs, which always bend, but never break; given a sound digestion, and a man in such training ought to live as long as the cedars of Lebanon, and famous trees they are.'

"'Then is the Count actually dying?' I asked.

"'That is possible,' said Gobseck; 'the winding up of his estate will be a juicy bit of business for you.'

"I looked at my man, and said, by way of sounding him:

"'Just explain to me how it is that we, the Count and I, are the only men in whom you take an interest?'

"'Because you are the only two who have trusted me without finessing,' he said.

"Although this answer warranted my belief that Gobseck would act fairly even if the counter-deed were lost, I resolved to go to see the Count. I pleaded a business engagement, and we separated.

"I went straight to the Rue du Helder, and was shown into a room where the Countess sat playing with her children. When she heard my name, she sprang up and came to meet me, then she sat down and pointed without a word to a chair by the fire. Her face wore the inscrutable mask beneath which women of the world conceal their most vehement emotions. Trouble had withered that face already. Nothing of its beauty now remained, save the marvelous outlines in which its principal charm had lain.

"'It is essential, madame, that I should speak to M. le Comte—'

"'If so, you would be more favored than I am,' she said, interrupting me. 'M. de Restaud will see no one. He will hardly allow his doctor to come, and will not be nursed even by me. When people are ill, they have such strange fancies! They are like children, they do not know what they want.'

"'Perhaps, like children, they know very well what they want.'

"The Countess reddened. I almost repented a thrust worthy of Gobseck. So, by way of changing the conversation, I added, 'But M. de Restaud cannot possibly lie there alone all day, madame.'

"'His oldest boy is with him,' she said.

"It was useless to gaze at the Countess; she did not blush this time, and it looked to me as if she were resolved more firmly than ever that I should not penetrate into her secrets.

"'You must understand, madame, that my proceeding is no way indiscreet. It is strongly to his interest—' I bit my lips, feeling that I had gone the wrong way to work. The Countess immediately took advantage of my slip.

"'My interests are in no way separate from my husband's, sir,' said she. 'There is nothing to prevent your addressing yourself to me——'

"'The business which brings me here concerns no one but M. le Comte,' I said firmly.

"'I will let him know of your wish to see him.'

"The civil tone and expression assumed for the occasion did not impose upon me; I divined that she would never allow me to see her husband. I chatted on about indifferent matters for a little while, so as to study her; but, like all women who have once begun to plot for themselves, she could dissimulate with the rare perfection which, in your sex, means the last degree of perfidy. If I may dare to say it, I looked for anything from her, even a crime. She produced this feeling in me, because it was so evident from her manner and in all that she did or said, down to the very inflections of her voice, that she had an eye to the future. I went.

"Now, I will pass on to the final scenes of this adventure,

throwing in a few circumstances brought to light by time, and some details guessed by Gobseck's perspicacity or by my own.

"When the Comte de Restaud apparently plunged into the vortex of dissipation, something passed between the husband and wife, something which remains an impenetrable secret, but the wife sank even lower in the husband's eyes. As soon as he became so ill that he was obliged to take to his bed, he manifested his aversion for the Countess and the two youngest children. He forbade them to enter his room, and any attempt to disobey his wishes brought on such dangerous attacks that the doctor implored the Countess to submit to her husband's wish.

"Mme. de Restaud had seen the family estates and property, nay, the very mansion in which she lived, pass into the hands of Gobseck, who appeared to play the fantastic ogre so far as their wealth was concerned. She partially understood what her husband was doing, no doubt. M. de Trailles was traveling in England (his creditors had been a little too pressing of late), and no one else was in a position to enlighten the lady, and explain that her husband was taking precautions against her at Gobseck's suggestion. It is said that she held out for a long while before she gave the signature required by French law for the sale of the property; nevertheless the Count gained his point. The Countess was convinced that her husband was realizing his fortune, and that somewhere or other there would be a little bunch of notes representing the amount; they had been deposited with a notary, or perhaps at the bank, or in some safe hiding-place. Following out her train of thought, it was evident that M. de Restaud must of necessity have some kind of document in his possession by which any remaining property could be recovered and handed over to his son.

"So she made up her mind to keep the strictest possible watch over the sick-room. She ruled despotically in the house, and everything in it was submitted to this feminine espionage. All day she sat in the salon adjoining her husband's room, so that she could hear every syllable that he uttered, every least movement that he made. She had a bed put there for her of a night, but she did not sleep very much. The doctor was entirely in her interests. Such wifely devotion seemed praiseworthy enough. With the natural subtlety of perfidy, she took care to disguise M. de Restaud's repugnance for her, and feigned distress so perfectly that she gained a sort of celebrity. Strait-laced women were even found to say that she had expiated her sins. Always before her eyes she beheld a vision of the destitution to follow on the Count's death if her presence of mind should fail her; and in these ways the wife, repulsed from the bed of pain on which her husband lay and groaned, had drawn a charmed circle round about it. So near, yet kept at a distance; all-powerful, but in disgrace, the apparently devoted wife was lying in wait for death and opportunity; crouching like the ant-lion at the bottom of his spiral pit, ever on the watch for the prey that cannot escape, listening to the fall of every grain of sand.

"The strictest censor could not but recognize that the Countess pushed maternal sentiment to the last degree. Her father's death had been a lesson to her, people said. She worshiped her children. They were so young that she could hide the disorders of her life from their eyes, and could win their love; she had given them the best and most brilliant education. I confess that I cannot help admiring her and feeling sorry for her. Gobseck used to joke me about it. Just about that time she had discovered Maxime's baseness, and was expiating the sins of the past in tears of blood. I was sure of it. Hateful as were the measures which she took for regaining control of her husband's money, were they not the result of a mother's love, and a desire to repair the wrongs she had done her children? And again, it may be, like many a woman who has experienced the storm of lawless love, she felt a longing to lead a virtuous life again. Perhaps she only learned the worth of that life when she came to reap the woeful harvest sown by her errors.

"Every time that little Ernest came out of his father's room, she put him through a searching examination as to all that his father had done or said. The boy willingly complied with his mother's wishes, and told her even more than she asked in her anxious affection, as he thought.

"My visit was a ray of light for the Countess. She was determined to see in me the instrument of the Count's vengeance, and resolved that I should not be allowed to go near the dying man.

I augured ill of all this, and earnestly wished for an interview, for I was not easy in my mind about the fate of the counter-deed. If it should fall into the Countess' hands, she might turn it to her own account, and that would be the beginning of a series of interminable lawsuits between her and Gobseck. I knew the usurer well enough to feel convinced that he would never give up the property to her; there was room for plenty of legal quibbling over a series of transfers, and I alone knew all the ins and outs of the matter. I was minded to prevent such a tissue of misfortune, so I went to the Countess a second time.

"I have noticed, madame," said Derville, turning to the Vicomtesse, and speaking in a confidential tone, "certain moral phenomena to which we do not pay enough attention. I am naturally an observer of human nature, and instinctively I bring a spirit of analysis to the business that I transact in the interest of others, when human passions are called into lively play. Now, I have often noticed, and always with new wonder, that two antagonists almost always divine each other's inmost thoughts and ideas. Two enemies sometimes possess a power of clear insight into mental processes, and read each other's minds as two lovers read in either soul. So when we came together, the Countess and I, I understood at once the reason of her antipathy for me, disguised though it was by the most gracious forms of politeness and civility. I had been forced to be her confidant, and a woman cannot but hate the man before whom she is compelled to blush. And she on her side knew that if I was the man in whom her husband placed confidence, that husband had not as yet given up his fortune.

"I will spare you the conversation, but it abides in my memory as one of the most dangerous encounters in my career. Nature had bestowed on her all the qualities which, combined, are irresistibly fascinating; she could be pliant and proud by turns, and confiding and coaxing in her manner; she even went so far as to try to subjugate me. It was a failure. As I took my leave of her, I caught a gleam of hate and rage in her eyes that made me shudder. We parted enemies. She would fain have crushed me out of existence; and for my own part, I felt pity for her, and for some natures pity is the deadliest of insults. This feeling pervaded the last representations I put before her; and when I left her, I left, I think, dread in the depths of her soul, by declaring that, turn which way she would, ruin lay inevitably before her.

"'If I were to see M. le Comte, your children's property at any rate would——'

"'I should be at your mercy,' she said, breaking in upon me, disgust in her gesture.

"Now that we had spoken frankly, I made up my mind to save the family from impending destitution. I resolved to strain the law at need to gain my ends, and this was what I did. I sued the Comte de Restaud for a sum of money, ostensibly due to Gobseck, and gained judgment. The Countess, of course, did not allow him to know of this, but I had gained on my point, I had a right to affix seals to everything on the death of the Count. I bribed one of the servants in the house—the man undertook to let me know at any hour of the day or night if his master should be at the point of death, so that I could intervene at once, scare the Countess with a threat of affixing seals, and so secure the counter-deed.

"I learned later on that the woman was studying the Code, with her husband's dying moans in her ears. If we could picture the thoughts of those who stand about a deathbed, what fearful sights should we not see? Money is always the motive-spring of the schemes elaborated, of all the plans that are made and the plots that are woven about it! Let us leave these details, nauseating in the nature of them; but perhaps they may have given you some insight into all that this husband and wife endured; perhaps too they may unveil much that is passing in secret in other houses.

"For two months the Comte de Restaud lay on his bed, alone, and resigned to his fate. Mortal disease was slowly sapping the strength of mind and body. Unaccountable and grotesque sick fancies preyed upon him; he would not suffer them to set his room in order, no one could nurse him, he would not even allow them to make his bed. All his surroundings bore the marks of this last degree of apathy, the furniture was out of place, the daintiest trifles were covered with dust and cobwebs. In health he had been a man of refined and expensive tastes, now he positively delighted in the comfortless look of the room. A host of objects required in illness—

rows of medicine bottles, empty and full, most of them dirty, crumpled linen, and broken plates, littered the writing-table, chairs, and chimney-piece. An open warming-pan lay on the floor before the grate; a bath, still full of mineral water had not been taken away. The sense of coming dissolution pervaded all the details of an unsightly chaos. Signs of death appeared in things inanimate before the Destroyer came to the body on the bed. The Comte de Restaud could not bear the daylight, the Venetian shutters were closed, darkness deepened the gloom in the dismal chamber. The sick man himself had wasted greatly. All the life in him seemed to have taken refuge in the still brilliant eyes. The livid whiteness of his face was something horrible to see, enhanced as it was by the long dank locks of hair that straggled along his cheeks, for he would never suffer them to cut it. He looked like some religious fanatic in the desert. Mental suffering was extinguishing all human instincts in this man of scarce fifty years of age, whom all Paris had known as so brilliant and so successful.

"One morning at the beginning of December 1824, he looked up at Ernest, who sat at the foot of his bed gazing at his father with wistful eyes.

"'Are you in pain?' the little Vicomte asked.

"'No,' said the Count, with a ghastly smile, 'it all lies here and about my heart!'

"He pointed to his forehead, and then laid his wasted fingers on his hollow chest. Ernest began to cry at the sight.

"'How is it that M. Derville does not come to me?' the Count asked his servant (he thought that Maurice was really attached to him, but the man was entirely in the Countess' interest)—'What! Maurice!' and the dying man suddenly sat upright in his bed, and seemed to recover all his presence of mind, 'I have sent for my attorney seven or eight times during the last fortnight, and he does not come!' he cried. 'Do you imagine that I am to be trifled with? Go for him, at once, this very instant, and bring him back with you. If you do not carry out my orders, I shall get up and go myself.'

"'Madame,' said the man as he came into the salon, 'you heard M. le Comte; what ought I to do?'

"'Pretend to go to the attorney, and when you come back tell your master that his man of business is forty leagues away from Paris on an important lawsuit. Say that he is expected back at the end of the week.—Sick people never know how ill they are,' thought the Countess; 'he will wait till the man comes home.'

"The doctor had said on the previous evening that the Count could scarcely live through the day. When the servant came back two hours later to give that hopeless answer, the dying man seemed to be greatly agitated.

"'Oh God!' he cried again and again, 'I put my trust in none but Thee.'

"For a long while he lay and gazed at his son, and spoke in a feeble voice at last.

"'Ernest, my boy, you are very young; but you have a good heart; you can understand, no doubt, that a promise given to a dying man is sacred; a promise to a father... Do you feel that you can be trusted with a secret, and keep it so well and so closely that even your mother herself shall not know that you have a secret to keep? There is no one else in this house whom I can trust to-day. You will not betray my trust, will you?'

"'No, father.'

"'Very well, then, Ernest, in a minute or two I will give you a sealed packet that belongs to M. Derville; you must take such care of it that no one can know that you have it; then you must slip out of the house and put the letter into the post-box at the corner.'

"'Yes, father.'

"'Can I depend upon you?'

"'Yes, father.'

"'Come and kiss me. You have made death less bitter to me, dear boy. In six or seven years' time you will understand the importance of this secret, and you will be well rewarded then for your quickness and obedience, you will know then how much I love you. Leave me alone for a minute, and let no one—no matter whom—come in meanwhile.'

"Ernest went out and saw his mother standing in the next room.

"'Ernest,' said she, 'come here.'

"She sat down, drew her son to her knees, and clasped him in her arms, and held him tightly to her heart.

"'Ernest, your father said something to you just now.'

"'Yes, mamma.'

"'What did he say?'

"'I cannot repeat it, mamma.'

"'Oh, my dear child!' cried the Countess, kissing him in rapture. 'You have kept your secret; how glad that makes me! Never tell a lie; never fail to keep your word—those are two principles which should never be forgotten.'

"'Oh! mamma, how beautiful you are! You have never told a lie, I am quite sure.'

"'Once or twice, Ernest dear, I have lied. Yes, and I have not kept my word under circumstances which speak louder than all precepts. Listen, my Ernest, you are big enough and intelligent enough to see that your father drives me away, and will not allow me to nurse him, and this is not natural, for you know how much I love him.'

"'Yes, mamma.'

"The Countess began to cry. 'Poor child!' she said, 'this misfortune is the result of treacherous insinuations. Wicked people have tried to separate me from your father to satisfy their greed. They mean to take all our money from us and to keep it for themselves. If your father were well, the division between us would soon be over; he would listen to me; he is loving and kind; he would see his mistake. But now his mind is affected, and his prejudices against me have become a fixed idea, a sort of mania with him. It is one result of his illness. Your father's fondness for you is another proof that his mind is deranged. Until he fell ill you never noticed that he loved you more than Pauline and Georges. It is all caprice with him now. In his affection for you he might take it into his head to tell you to do things for him. If you do not want to ruin us all, my darling, and to see your mother begging her bread like a pauper woman, you must tell her everything——'

"'Ah!' cried the Count. He had opened the door and stood there, a sudden, half-naked apparition, almost as thin and fleshless as a skeleton.

"His smothered cry produced a terrible effect upon the Countess; she sat motionless, as if a sudden stupor had seized her. Her husband was as white and wasted as if he had risen out of his grave.

"'You have filled my life to the full with trouble, and now you are trying to vex my deathbed, to warp my boy's mind, and make a depraved man of him!' he cried, hoarsely.

"The Countess flung herself at his feet. His face, working with the last emotions of life, was almost hideous to see.

"'Mercy! mercy!' she cried aloud, shedding a torrent of tears.

"'Have you shown me any pity?' he asked. 'I allowed you to squander your own money, and now do you mean to squander my fortune, too, and ruin my son?'

"'Ah! well, yes, have no pity for me, be merciless to me!' she cried. 'But the children? Condemn your widow to live in a convent; I will obey you; I will do anything, anything that you bid me, to expiate the wrong I have done you, if that so the children may be happy! The children! Oh, the children!'

"'I have only one child,' said the Count, stretching out a wasted arm, in his despair, towards his son.

"'Pardon a penitent woman, a penitent woman!...' wailed the Countess, her arms about her husband's damp feet. She could not speak for sobbing; vague, incoherent sounds broke from her parched throat.

"'You dare to talk of penitence after all that you said to Ernest!' exclaimed the dying man, shaking off the Countess, who lay groveling over his feet.—'You turn me to ice!' he added, and there was something appalling in the indifference with which he uttered the words. 'You have been a bad daughter; you have been a bad wife; you will be a bad mother.'

"The wretched woman fainted away. The dying man reached his bed and lay down again, and a few hours later sank into unconsciousness. The priests came and administered the sacraments.

"At midnight he died; the scene that morning had exhausted his remaining strength, and on the stroke of midnight I arrived with Daddy Gobseck. The house was in confusion, and under cover of it

155

we walked up into the little salon adjoining the death-chamber. The three children were there in tears, with two priests, who had come to watch with the dead. Ernest came over to me, and said that his mother desired to be alone in the Count's room.

"'Do not go in,' he said; and I admired the child for his tone and gesture; 'she is praying there.'

"Gobseck began to laugh that soundless laugh of his, but I felt too much touched by the feeling in Ernest's little face to join in the miser's sardonic amusement. When Ernest saw that we moved towards the door, he planted himself in front of it, crying out, 'Mamma, here are some gentlemen in black who want to see you!'

"Gobseck lifted Ernest out of the way as if the child had been a feather, and opened the door.

"What a scene it was that met our eyes! The room was in frightful disorder; clothes and papers and rags lay tossed about in a confusion horrible to see in the presence of Death; and there, in the midst, stood the Countess in disheveled despair, unable to utter a word, her eyes glittering. The Count had scarcely breathed his last before his wife came in and forced open the drawers and the desk; the carpet was strewn with litter, some of the furniture and boxes were broken, the signs of violence could be seen everywhere. But if her search had at first proved fruitless, there was that in her excitement and attitude which led me to believe that she had found the mysterious documents at last. I glanced at the bed, and professional instinct told me all that had happened. The mattress had been flung contemptuously down by the bedside, and across it, face downwards, lay the body of the Count, like one of the paper envelopes that strewed the carpet—he too was nothing now but an envelope. There was something grotesquely horrible in the attitude of the stiffening rigid limbs.

"The dying man must have hidden the counter-deed under his pillow to keep it safe so long as life should last; and his wife must have guessed his thought; indeed, it might be read plainly in his last dying gesture, in the convulsive clutch of his claw-like hands. The pillow had been flung to the floor at the foot of the bed; I could see the print of her heel upon it. At her feet lay a paper with the Count's arms on the seals; I snatched it up, and saw that it was addressed to me. I looked steadily at the Countess with the pitiless clear-sightedness of an examining magistrate confronting a guilty creature. The contents were blazing in the grate; she had flung them on the fire at the sound of our approach, imagining, from a first hasty glance at the provisions which I had suggested for her children, that she was destroying a will which disinherited them. A tormented conscience and involuntary horror of the deed which she had done had taken away all power of reflection. She had been caught in the act, and possibly the scaffold was rising before her eyes, and she already felt the felon's branding iron.

"There she stood gasping for breath, waiting for us to speak, staring at us with haggard eyes.

"I went across to the grate and pulled out an unburned fragment. 'Ah, madame!' I exclaimed, 'you have ruined your children! Those papers were their titles to their property.'

"Her mouth twitched, she looked as if she were threatened by a paralytic seizure.

"'Eh! eh!' cried Gobseck; the harsh, shrill tone grated upon our ears like the sound of a brass candlestick scratching a marble surface.

"There was a pause, then the old man turned to me and said quietly:

"'Do you intend Mme. la Comtesse to suppose that I am not the rightful owner of the property sold to me by her late husband? This house belongs to me now.'

"A sudden blow on the head from a bludgeon would have given me less pain and astonishment. The Countess saw the look of hesitation in my face.

"'Monsieur,' she cried, 'Monsieur!' She could find no other words.

"'You are a trustee, are you not?' I asked.

"'That is possible.'

"'Then do you mean to take advantage of this crime of hers?'

"'Precisely.'

"I went at that, leaving the Countess sitting by her husband's bedside, shedding hot tears. Gobseck followed me. Outside in the street I separated from him, but he came after me, flung me one of those searching glances with which he probed men's minds, and said in the husky flute-tones, pitched in a shriller key:

"'Do you take it upon yourself to judge me?'"

"From that time forward we saw little of each other. Gobseck let the Count's mansion on lease; he spent the summers on the country estates. He was a lord of the manor in earnest, putting up farm buildings, repairing mills and roadways, and planting timber. I came across him one day in a walk in the Jardin des Tuileries.

"'The Countess is behaving like a heroine,' said I; 'she gives herself up entirely to the children's education; she is giving them a perfect bringing up. The oldest boy is a charming young fellow—'

"'That is possible.'

"'But ought you not to help Ernest?' I suggested.

"'Help him!' cried Gobseck. 'Not I. Adversity is the greatest of all teachers; adversity teaches us to know the value of money and the worth of men and women. Let him set sail on the seas of Paris; when he is a qualified pilot, we will give him a ship to steer.'

"I left him without seeking to explain the meaning of his words.

"M. de Restaud's mother has prejudiced him against me, and he is very far from taking me as his legal adviser; still, I went to see Gobseck last week to tell him about Ernest's love for Mlle. Camille, and pressed him to carry out his contract, since that young Restaud is just of age.

"I found the old bill-discounter had been kept to his bed for a long time by the complaint of which he was to die. He put me off, saying that he would give the matter his attention when he could get up again and see after his business; his idea being no doubt that he would not give up any of his possessions so long as the breath was in him; no other reason could be found for his shuffling answer. He seemed to me to be much worse than he at all suspected. I stayed with him long enough to discern the progress of a passion which age had converted into a sort of craze. He wanted to be alone in the house, and had taken the rooms one by one as they fell vacant. In his own room he had changed nothing; the furniture which I knew so well sixteen years ago looked the same as ever; it might have been kept under a glass case. Gobseck's faithful old portress, with her husband, a pensioner, who sat in the entry while she was upstairs, was still his housekeeper and charwoman, and now in addition his sick-nurse. In spite of his feebleness, Gobseck saw his clients himself as heretofore, and received sums of money; his affairs had been so simplified, that he only needed to send his pensioner out now and again on an errand, and could carry on business in his bed.

"After the treaty, by which France recognized the Haytian Republic, Gobseck was one of the members of the commission appointed to liquidate claims and assess repayments due by Hayti; his special knowledge of old fortunes in San Domingo, and the planters and their heirs and assigns to whom the indemnities were due, had led to his nomination. Gobseck's peculiar genius had then devised an agency for discounting the planters' claims on the government. The business was carried on under the names of Werbrust and Gigonnet, with whom he shared the spoil without disbursements, for his knowledge was accepted instead of capital. The agency was a sort of distillery, in which money was extracted from doubtful claims, and the claims of those who knew no better, or had no confidence in the government. As a liquidator, Gobseck could make terms with the large landed proprietors; and these, either to gain a higher percentage of their claims, or to ensure prompt settlements, would send him presents in proportion to their means. In this way presents came to be a kind of percentage upon sums too large to pass through his control, while the agency bought up cheaply the small and dubious claims, or the claims of those persons who preferred a little ready money to a deferred and somewhat hazy repayment by the Republic. Gobseck was the insatiable boa constrictor of the great business. Every morning he received his tribute, eyeing it like a Nabob's prime minister, as he considers whether he will sign a pardon. Gobseck would take anything, from the present of game sent him by some poor devil or the pound's weight of wax candles from devout folk, to the rich man's plate and the speculator's gold snuff-box. Nobody knew what became of the presents sent to the old money-lender. Everything went in, but nothing came out.

"'On the word of an honest woman,' said the portress, an old acquaintance of mine, 'I believe he swallows it all and is none the fatter for it; he is as thin and dried up as the cuckoo in the clock.'

"At length, last Monday, Gobseck sent his pensioner for me. The man came up to my private office.

"'Be quick and come, M. Derville,' said he, 'the governor is just going to hand in his checks; he has grown as yellow as a lemon; he is fidgeting to speak with you; death has fair hold of him; the rattle is working in his throat.'

"When I entered Gobseck's room, I found the dying man kneeling before the grate. If there was no fire on the hearth, there was at any rate a monstrous heap of ashes. He had dragged himself out of bed, but his strength had failed him, and he could neither go back nor find the voice to complain.

"'You felt cold, old friend,' I said, as I helped him back to his bed; 'how can you do without a fire?'

"'I am not cold at all,' he said. 'No fire here! no fire! I am going, I know not where, lad,' he went on, glancing at me with blank, lightless eyes, 'but I am going away from this.—I have carpology,' said he (the use of the technical term showing how clear and accurate his mental processes were even now). 'I thought the room was full of live gold, and I got up to catch some of it.—To whom will all mine go, I wonder? Not to the crown; I have left a will, look for it, Grotius. La belle Hollandaise had a daughter; I once saw the girl somewhere or other, in the Rue Vivienne, one evening. They call her "La Torpille," I believe; she is as pretty as pretty can be; look her up, Grotius. You are my executor; take what you like; help yourself. There are Strasburg pies, there, and bags of coffee, and sugar, and gold spoons. Give the Odiot service to your wife. But who is to have the diamonds? Are you going to take them, lad? There is snuff too—sell it at Hamburg, tobaccos are worth half as much again at Hamburg. All sorts of things I have in fact, and now I must go and leave them all.—Come, Papa Gobseck, no weakness, be yourself!'

"He raised himself in bed, the lines of his face standing out as sharply against the pillow as if the profile had been cast in bronze; he stretched out a lean arm and bony hand along the coverlet and clutched it, as if so he would fain keep his hold on life, then he gazed hard at the grate, cold as his own metallic eyes, and died in full consciousness of death. To us—the portress, the old pensioner, and myself—he looked like one of the old Romans standing behind the Consuls in Lethiere's picture of the Death of the Sons of Brutus.

"'He was a good-plucked one, the old Lascar!' said the pensioner in his soldierly fashion.

"But as for me, the dying man's fantastical enumeration of his riches still sounding in my ears, and my eyes, following the direction of his, rested on that heap of ashes. It struck me that it was very large. I took the tongs, and as soon as I stirred the cinders, I felt the metal underneath, a mass of gold and silver coins, receipts taken during his illness, doubtless, after he grew too feeble to lock the money up, and could trust no one to take it to the bank for him.

"'Run for the justice of the peace,' said I, turning to the old pensioner, 'so that everything can be sealed here at once.'

"Gobseck's last words and the old portress' remarks had struck me. I took the keys of the rooms on the first and second floor to make a visitation. The first door that I opened revealed the meaning of the phrases which I took for mad ravings; and I saw the length to which covetousness goes when it survives only as an illogical instinct, the last stage of greed of which you find so many examples among misers in country towns.

"In the room next to the one in which Gobseck had died, a quantity of eatables of all kinds were stored—putrid pies, mouldy fish, nay, even shell-fish, the stench almost choked me. Maggots and insects swarmed. These comparatively recent presents were put down, pell-mell, among chests of tea, bags of coffee, and packing-cases of every shape. A silver soup tureen on the chimney-piece was full of advices of the arrival of goods consigned to his order at Havre, bales of cotton, hogsheads of sugar, barrels of rum, coffees, indigo, tobaccos, a perfect bazaar of colonial produce. The room itself was crammed with furniture, and silver-plate, and lamps, and vases, and pictures; there were books, and curiosities, and fine engravings lying rolled up, unframed. Perhaps these were not all presents, and some part of this vast quantity of stuff had been deposited with him in the shape of pledges, and had been left on his hands in default of payment. I noticed jewel-cases, with ciphers and armorial bearings stamped upon them, and sets of fine table-linen, and weapons of price; but none of the things were docketed. I opened a book which seemed to be misplaced, and found a thousand-franc note in it. I promised myself that I would go through everything thoroughly; I would try the ceilings, and floors, and walls, and cornices to discover all the gold, hoarded with such passionate greed by a Dutch miser worthy of a Rembrandt's brush. In all the course of my professional career I have never seen such impressive signs of the eccentricity of avarice.

"I went back to his room, and found an explanation of this chaos and accumulation of riches in a pile of letters lying under the paper-weights on his desk—Gobseck's correspondence with the various dealers to whom doubtless he usually sold his presents. These persons had, perhaps, fallen victims to Gobseck's cleverness, or Gobseck may have wanted fancy prices for his goods; at any rate, every bargain hung in suspense. He had not disposed of the eatables to Chevet, because Chevet would only take them of him at a loss of thirty per cent. Gobseck haggled for a few francs between the prices, and while they wrangled the goods became unsalable. Again, Gobseck had refused free delivery of his silver-plate, and declined to guarantee the weights of his coffees. There had been a dispute over each article, the first indication in Gobseck of the childishness and incomprehensible obstinacy of age, a condition of mind reached at last by all men in whom a strong passion survives the intellect.

"I said to myself, as he had said, 'To whom will all these riches go?' ... And then I think of the grotesque information he gave me as to the present address of his heiress, I foresee that it will be my duty to search all the houses of ill-fame in Paris to pour out an immense fortune on some worthless jade. But, in the first place, know this— that in a few days time Ernest de Restaud will come into a fortune to which his title is unquestionable, a fortune which will put him in a position to marry Mlle. Camille, even after adequate provision has been made for his mother the Comtesse de Restaud and his sister and brother."

THE END